Artemis and The Dating App

The Queer Olympus Goddesses, Volume 1

Carly Cane

Published by Carly Cane, 2020.

ARTEMIS AND THE DATING APP

First edition. January 23, 2020.

Written by Carly Cane.

To H,

My very own Queer Goddess

2000 years earlier...

The night was wrapped around us like a star-dotted blanket, smoothing out the edges of Callisto's features into the dark shadows. Not a single blade of light reached our tiny alcove - a knotted carpet of roots and crisp leafs at the base of an ancient oak tree.

"You promised to love me forever, didn't you? / So don't mind me, if I do too"

Dionysus' serenading of his new bride was the only sound easily heard across the entire woods.

"I find this celebration a bit excessive," I said as I leaned against the coarse tree trunk. The spiky chips of wood pinched my back. The position offered me a fully enchanting view of Callisto's smile.

She arched her eyebrows. "Oh really?"

"Really. He loves her, we get it. Have a bit of stoicism, please."

Her sparkly eyes, hazy with tipsiness, danced over mine. "Oh Please, Goddess of the Hunt, show me that stoicism of yours, I seem to have forgotten." She looked irresistible when she teased me. I suspected she knew that much.

I tackled her to the ground, feeling her quickened heartbeat against mine behind the soft curve of her chest.

"I am very stoic," I growled in her ear.

"Sure," she commented. I could feel her smile against my earlobe.

"Say I'm stoic."

"Never."

1

"What impertinence," I nibbled her neck and a soft moan escaped her lips.

"I cannot lie to a Goddess," she said in a breathless voice.

I liked that. My hand grazed her leg and her breath hitched. "Say I'm very stoic," I whispered again.

"I love you because you're *not* stoic with me...".

"Fine then, I'll go grab more ambrosia, if you insist on being so bull headed." I fell back onto my heels and stood up.

"And leave me here all alone in the woods?" she said with a smirk.

I hesitated. Splayed on the ground, in her white tunic and with her wild hair framing her face, it seemed too good of a chance to pass up. We did need a refill, though. "I'll be back soon," I reassured her.

"Please do."

A new swell of warmth spread inside my chest. I didn't even know I could love anyone, let alone this much. I threw her one last smile. "Will do."

I dragged my eyes away from her and took a few unsteady steps on the meandering path that led towards the celebration meadow.

"*And never shall I wish on someone new/ when I have you in my arms, boo*"

Goddess. This was getting worse by the second.

Still, I *was* smiling like an idiot. I was planning a similar celebration for Callisto and I, my Father be damned. If he had a problem with it, we'd know soon enough. For now, I just wanted to keep it a surprise from Callisto.

I found the wine barrell in the center of the party and, ignoring the crowd around me, refilled the jug I was carrying.

"Hey you!" The nymph's eyes darted on me brimming with ecstasy. "Haven't seen you in a while.."

"I don't remember you-"

A pair of goat heels dug into my feet, and the faun they belonged to fell into my arms before I had realised what had happened.

He took a look at my expression. "I'm sorry, I'm sorry." He scrambled away.

"Eleana... The night at the beach." The nymph yelled across the festive uproar.

My mind kept drawing a blank, I couldn't remember any of the beaches I'd been to.

"Was I that forgettable?" she said with a pout.

"Comingggg." A centaur galloped past us with two barrels of wine balanced on his shoulders.

"Of course not, I just happen to have a terrible memory. If you'll excuse me now."

"Please don't go, we've only just started." She gripped my arm and snuggled my hand between the soft mounds of her cleavage.

Enough. I untangled my hand. "I'm going now. But you see that nymph over there?" I pointed to my tall, prickly nymph. "Her name is Nerea, and she'll be tremendously pleased with your attention."

The nymph followed the direction of my finger. "Nice."

"Good luck."

The nymph's hair jumped off her shoulders as she rushed through the meadow calling Nerea's name.

I sighed. It was a great night. Superb.

I stumbled down the dark path smiling like an idiot with a full jug of ambrosia in my hand.

A couple more strides into the woods and the power of the flame-light had completely given up.

"Where are you?" I called into the wind, barely above a whisper.

There was no answer.

I took a few more unsteady steps and my heart leaped at the thought of a dark premonition. I steadied my breath: *it was a good night, a celebration, everything was alright.*

I went deeper into the woods.

The sound of moaning reached me when I was halfway to our spot. My blood turned cold.

I'd recognise that sound anywhere.

The world started spinning and I darted forward towards Callisto as fast as my drunken legs would allow me.

She was there, with her eyes closed and her breath hitched.

But the person on top of her wasn't me.

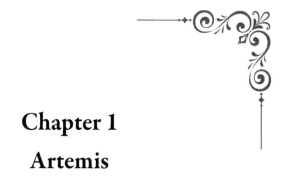

Chapter 1
Artemis

"YOU'RE A DIRTY LITTLE perv, aren't you? Oh yes, I know you are."

Aphrodite was splayed on the chaise longue, staring intently at the device in her hand while chewing on her thumb. "I could make a cushion out of your dimples. Oh yes, I could."

I did my best to ignore her.

"Oh dear! He sent me a picture of his penis! Can you believe it?" Her laugh sent the glasses at the banquet rattling with a nervous jingle. "Artemis, come and see this."

"... No, thank you." I pulled at the string of my bow. Before I could tie it around its end, the string snapped and whipped my hand. Hard. "Fucking Hades."

"You don't want to see the humans' new toy?" she waved the device in front of my face, "it's hilarious."

"Aphrodite. I told you, I don't give a -"

"What is it?" Athena peeked at us from behind her book.

"It's a library of humans at the tip of your fingertips, where anyone can go through the pictures and decide whether each person is attractive for their taste," this time she aimed the bright screen in our sister's direction.

I sighed, loudly enough that it would get on her nerves. "How idiotic."

Athena fell back on her book, "I suppose it's a slightly more efficient method to find a suitable life partner."

I rolled my eyes at her democratic answer. "It's a waste of time."

"Oh but it's so much fun, look!" Aphrodite said, relentless. "I like," her thumb swiped at the screen, "I don't like."

"As I said.." I shot a glance in her direction, "it's ridiculous."

"Oh Artie, loneliness really *is* a terrible look on you." She shook her head. "If you smiled more you'd look prettier and then perhaps you'd get some much needed attention."

I steeled my gaze. Had I been able to take the immortal life of my sister, I would have.

A long time ago.

"I don't care about *prettiness*, Aphrodite. And love is a lie, so I see no need to put myself through ridiculous human mating rituals."

"Love is a lie, huh?" My sister was carefully staring at her nails, that were painted with a headache-inducing shade of pink.

"Of course," I said, "it's just lust destined to turn into ashes when difficulties arise." My eyes were glued to the floor.

"Is this just your personal experience, perhaps?"

"No, it's a fact."

"It's curious that you mentioned that, because I found a certain Hanna in here that looks exactly like someone we both know," she said.

I tried to keep my face composed. "Oh?"

"Her name was Callisto before," she said, "does it ring any bells, sis?"

Callisto.

The device sat casually on my sister's lap but the glint in her eyes betrayed her excitement.

In the space of a human blink I lunged towards my sister, my arm outstretched in a desperate effort to reach the black object.

The rectangle disappeared behind Aphrodite's dress, hidden in the many folds that swirled around her legs.

"Give it to me, Aphrodite."

"Nope," she said, throwing me a smug smile, as if she were a human child of three instead of a Goddess of Mount Olympus who had been celebrated by poets of all reputations and magnitudes for millenia.

"Aphrodite." The promise of retaliation coated every syllable of her name.

My sister pretended not to hear.

I gave a long, dramatic sigh and fell back on the sofa. "It's probably not even her." I picked up my bow again. "How could she be on Earth? It must be someone else."

"Father must have sent her back to Earth to have some more fun."

My stomach lurched, threatening to empty its content right there and then.

"But how lucky you are for not caring, sister!" Aphrodite said in her sing-song voice. "Remember? Love doesn't even exist!"

I took advantage of her distraction and lunged at her again. This time I missed the black device but we both tumbled down on the soft carpet under her recliner. I grabbed at her hand and turned it towards me.

HANNA

6,532 miles away

I like the outdoors, dogs and marshmallow roasting on a campfire. I've been on a bad-girls rehab program, and I am now looking for a serious relationship.

THE PICTURE WAS UNMISTAKABLY Callisto. Her curly hair and caramel skin looked as soft as I remembered. The eyes, her smile. A pang of sadness pooled at my stomach. "Yeah, I remember her," I said, fighting to appear unfazed.

"So you stand by your words that love does not exist?"

I raised my gaze to hers. "Yes. Of course."

"Fantastic!" My sister jumped up. She blew one of her waves away from her face and settled her dress back in place. "Then prove it!"

"I am a Goddess of Olympus, I don't need to prove anything at all. Plus," I said with the intent of wiping that smug smile from her face, "I think you should be the one proving your knowledge on the matter of Love. From where I'm standing, you seem to know very little on the matter."

That did it. Her smile was replaced by a frown. It was an unusual sight: my sister was usually too concerned about wrinkles.

"Excuse me?"

"You are the Goddess of Eros, carnal love, yet you've never experienced such a thing with a woman, or a female divine creature, have you?"

"Because it doesn't count!" She replied, indignant.

"Oh really, so you believe the tales about my supposed virginity?"

"No, of course not. It's just-" Aphrodite said.

"Then you are not really any good as the Goddess of Eros, are you?"

Athena cleared her throat, oblivious as always to the gravity of the situation. "Frankly, I find the binary gender separation you are all imposing on this conversation offensive and archaic...-"

"-Right. I forgot I had a *virgin* sister with extensive knowledge about human queer theory but no apparent business in the community." My face conveyed the precise shade of disbelief I felt at that concept.

"I'm *in fact* a virgin" Athena said, with a displeased attitude, "and I am attracted to knowledge of all kinds."

"Uh-huh."

"So it looks like I have two sisters who refuse to accept that love and eros are part of everyone's experience..." Aphrodite's features had settled back into the maddening, euphoric look she typically paraded around.

"Three," I said. "Since you are still very ignorant of the other half of love." My stomach had not settled yet from the memory of Callisto.

"Very well, then-" my sister fell back on the tryclinium, arranging her skirt to fall off the velvety cushions *just so*. "I hereby declare a wager."

"Absolutely n-"

"You, sister," she pointed at me, "will spend two weeks with Callisto in a location of my choosing. Should you fall *back* in love, you will live a human life and exist as one of them with no powers to rely on."

"And why would I accept that?" I asked.

"Because otherwise I'll point Father straight to Callisto."

The pain in my stomach crackled like a fire. "Why would you do that?"

"I am the Goddess of love and you dare question my judgement?"

The fire exploded behind my eyes, "I am the Goddess of the Hunt and I will stalk you until the end of times if you insist on threatening me."

Aphrodite's smile vanished. "Wait, don't be in such haste. I see you have a point there. The truth is I have not experienced carnal desire and love for a woman. You seem adamant that I could, though, that's why I saw an opportunity for a bet."

"What would your side of it be?" I asked cautiously.

"I will choose Callisto for you and you'll choose someone from the device for me in turn. A woman specifically. And if I were to fall in love with this person, not only would you be returned to Olympus right away, but you'll also have the right to brag about defeating the Goddess of Love for the rest of eternity."

"Absolutely -"

"Plus, love is a lie, isn't it sister?" She said, incapable of recognising when it was time to shut up.

Right that moment, I hated her smug smile. Hated it. She thought she knew better than me, she thought she understood love better than me. She'd never known what it was like to wake up with a pool of sweat and a empty heart night after night.

I also knew she'd cast her bait and I wasn't going to fall for it. No way.

"I'll get you the bow to replace the one you can't fix," Aphrodite broke the silence.

"What?"

"I'll ask Father for it myself. And I'll make sure no human will ever enter your woods again."

"Nobody has that power."

"Zeus does."

"We both know Father is too obsessed by his little human creations to stop them from roaming around to their hearts' desire."

"I have something - well, someone - he wants. I'll offer a trade-"

My woods. The second thing I'd lost.

"-I accept." My mouth spoke of its own accord.

Aphrodite smiled. It was the kind of cheshire smile that proved that there was as much wickedness in her as there was beauty. Poor artists, they had no idea who they'd been celebrating.

This time, though, she was wrong.

I didn't care about Callisto anymore, especially as a human. This was going to be the safest bet I'd ever won. I would get back everything I used to love: roaming the uncontaminated woods with my nymphs, the dogs and our hunting trips, sleeping on the open ground, the stars above us. I would no longer be a prisoner. I would no longer have to obey my Father's rules. It would be perfect, it would be exactly like it used to be...

"I'll be the wager arbiter," Athena said, interrupting my thoughts.

We both looked at her, frowning. "You know absolutely nothing of Love. How could you possibly be an appropriate judge for such a wager?"

Athena looked at the two of us as if we were mad. "My impartiality is exactly what makes me a great judge."

"Maybe you just haven't found the right human..." Aphrodite said, with a wicked smile on her lips. "The only way to test your absolute impartiality is by making you participate in the wager as well. This way we'll see if you are truly capable of resisting the allure of Love."

"Please," Athena said, looking at the two of us as if we struggled with basic logical concepts. "I have resisted it for millennia."

Aphrodite was not set back. "Humans have improved in the past thousands of years, I think we'll find the right person for you."

"Woman," I corrected her.

"Woman, of course," Aphrodite smiled.

"And why would I get entangled in this, exactly?" Athena asked, looking at us with the exact exasperated expression she usually reserved for Aphrodite's poorly constructed plans.

"Don't you want to be heralded by the new poets as the most invulnerable of the Goddesses? And what is more vulnerable and human than love? It should be so easy for you.." Aphrodite suggested.

Athena's stoney expression did not change. "It will be," she said.

"So, it's been decided then," Aphrodite said.

"Right," I said reaching for the rectangular object, "it's my turn to play now."

"What are you looking for?" A shadow of fear hung in my sister's voice.

This was going to be so good.

"A bull-dyke of course." I smiled wickedly as I flicked through the faces. "A badass butch to keep you in your place."

"That sounds terrifying."

"..and a lot of fun for me," I said, unable to suppress the joy I felt in thinking of myself sister on Earth, bending to the will of a powerful woman.

I continued wading through pictures of different humans, all terribly basic, until I came across a woman who looked absolutely perfect. Vik. 35. With a motorcycle in the background and a stance for a man to fear. I knew my sister well enough to recognise the woman that would work on her.

I handed over the device to my sister, "you're welcome."

She studied the picture for a while. I saw a hint of curiosity, then interest. She hid it soon enough. "I will win this bet," she declared at last.

"What about me?" Athena asked.

Aphrodite and I looked at each other. A flash of understanding passed between us and I knew what I had to do.

I quickly brushed past a few profiles and handed the phone to my sister.

The screen read:

MAGDALENA. 38.

College professor living in a small college town. I am about to complete my magna opera on the role of gender through history.

ATHENA'S EYES WIDENED as she looked at both of us. "How is it even-?"

"I told you, humans have become quite intelligent," Aphrodite said, "they are now capable of showing humans from the library that could be of most interest, first."

It was clear that Athena did not believe the lazy lie. But, still, she kept quiet. Her interest in working with the woman was clearly affecting her judgement.

She threw one last sideways glance at us and then nodded.

"It has been decided then," Aphrodite said with finality to her words. We held each other's fists and swore a solemn oath to seal the pact.

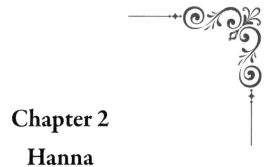

Chapter 2
Hanna

THE BRIGHT SCREEN OF my phone informed me that it was 1 am.

I unlocked the front door quietly, desperate to take my heels off and dive into bed.

"It's late and you're wet," was Lori's matter-of-fact greeting. "You must have had way more fun on your date than I gave you credit for."

I dumped the keys in the general direction of our miscellaneous bowl. Droplets of water cascaded from my jacket to the floor and every step produced a small puddle on the hardwood floor. "I would describe it more like *soaked*."

"Are you saying that this..." Lori gestured at my clothes, "..was not because of a date gone really, really well?"

"Lori, let me ask you, do you know anything about women's anatomy?"

"Not as much as I should probably," she plopped back on the sofa while I went to change.

"So what happened?" she asked once I was finally dry and splayed on the sofa in my pyjamas.

"Emergency at the clinic. A pipe broke and the entire floor is under 10 inches of water. Worst part is that the technician won't be here until next week."

"Shoot."

"They're going to have to close for the next two weeks, at least, I'd say. The regulations are just so strict about the conditions for the animals. I mean, rightfully so, obviously. I just don't know how I'm going to work in the meantime."

"Free vacation. Yay!" Lori handed me over the packet of monster munch. "Don't worry about having too much free-time, I can send you on two dates a day this way!"

"Honestly, after this one..."

"So it wasn't good?"

I looked at her deflated. "Does this look like the face of someone who had fun?"

Her crisps-filled hand stopped mid-way to her mouth. "No?" She asked, looking disappointed.

I shook my head slowly, reaching for the crisps in her open palm "I blame you" I said, stuffing my mouth with the two I managed to sneak "it's either that, or there is a God up there who really hates me"

I tried to reach for another crisp but Lori snatched her hand away from me.

"I thought we were friends" I said, eyeing the bag of crisps in her other hand.

"Not around monster munch." She said soberly "when it comes to crisps, we are strangers who barely tolerate each other".

I took a deep sigh "Fine."

I adjusted my own position on the sofa and let my aching back sink into the knobby cushions. I rested there for a moment and felt a wave of relief pass over me as I closed my eyes.

Opening them again, I found a big bowl of crisps sitting on my lap and Lori grinning at me from the nearby kitchen.

"You are the best." I said, taking a deep breath "Any chance I could get a massage as well?" I asked hopefully.

"You're testing your luck, now, babe" she said.

"Fair enough". Lori joined me on the sofa again and I leaned my head towards her, my neck stretched against the coarse fabric of the sofa. I passed the bowl in her direction before taking a large handful.

"So?" She asked.

"So...why did you even make me download the damn thing?"

"It's been a year. You need to go out there and force yourself to meet someone new."

Finley was still too much of a vivid presence in the tiny apartment. Lori and I never mentioned her, not by name at least, but the shadow of what she had done still managed to seep through every conversation we shared.

"Why?" I asked, looking at her from my sideways position. "What if I want to be alone?"

"Look, babe" she said "we've been through all the phases, times and times again. Denial, isolation, watching Lip Service on repeat, anger. And there are only so many more times I can see you mouth the lines to the screen. It's sad. Also, the best way I know to get to the acceptance stage is to get you out there and meeting people. Multiple people. People who live in the real world who you can interact with."

Lori's plan may have seemed perfectly reasonable except for one major detail "It's not like she's dead." I said "She's probably with her *colleague* sipping margaritas in Aruba," I said, sounding more bitter than I wanted to. I truly didn't feel like I cared about Finley anymore, it was Aruba that I wished I could enjoy.

Lori gave me a searching look, ignoring my well-thought out point.

"I think the problem might be you, honestly," she declared at last.

Lori had been my best friend since college and I usually enjoyed her bluntness, but this time she was wrong.

I gave her my best side eye. "I can tell you what tonight's candidate for Mrs. Right did. Perhaps that will finally convince you you're wrong."

"Yes please" she said, excited again. "Tell me everything. How bad it was on a scale from 1 to 10?"

"She was charming and lovely. Everything was going great. Except when I got the call from the vet about the broken pipe, she just excused herself to the bathroom and left without saying goodbye. Yep, yep I know." I said, seeing Lori's outraged expression. "Wait for it. It gets worse. While I was knee deep in sewage water, two hours later, I received a message saying '*Becky doesn't like liars*.'"

"Who's Becky?! I thought her name was Jordan"

"Becky is her dog."

"Do you think she has a telepathic connection to animals? That could be really useful for a vet.."

"I highly doubt it." I said, passing on the crisps. "Either way, I am not going to stick around to find out. It was a touch too weird for me."

"Mmm .. I see" Lori said suddenly pensieve, chomping on another handful of crisps "It is a weird name for a dog.."

"Lori, the dog's name was the least bit of the problem."

"I mean, I am not the best connoisseur of lesbian dating, so I didn't want to make assumptions about what would constitute normalcy in a dating scenario..." her voice trailed off when she took a look at my expression. "Well, did you at least bond over heartbreak?"

I threw the pillow at her smug face. "I told you. I'm over Finley."

"Is that why you still have a strict ban on muscly, butch women with tattoos?" She asked, throwing the pillow back at me.

"It has nothing to do with that," I insisted, "I think I should just try different types, before settling for one specific one".

"You can't tell your vagina what to like anymore that you can command your heart, babe. And I am afraid this is true of every gender and sexuality."

"I do command my vagina enough to know that there is no way I am going for the bad girl type again. I want sweet. Vanilla and honey level of sweet. Custard level of sweet. White chocolate. And there are clearly no butches that follow this description."

"First of all, thank you very much for making me hungry."

"You're welcome."

"Second, you're wrong." I shot her a look. "And let's say you're right. It doesn't matter! No one's asking you to move in with anyone. You could just have a bit of fun" she said, with her signature wiggly eyebrow "The sex kind." she added for good measure.

"I knew what you meant."

"Hence why I got the app for you. And somehow you still manage to use it wrong." She said, munching on more crisps. "Honestly you're hopeless".

Unfortunately for me, Lori revived her hope quite quickly. I saw the light bulb turn on in her head. "You know what? I think it's time for us to stop looking at the past and focus on the future" Lori announced. She grabbed her phone.

Disarmed by the abrupt change in tone, I was not prepared when she shoved a picture of a woman under my nose "I found this girl. Look at her."

The woman in the picture had full pink lips and her bio read "Send me a dad-pun and I'll fuck you against a wall".

"Whew. Sounds like exactly what I need" I said sarcastically.

"I know" Lori said enthusiastically and seemingly oblivious to my sarcasm "I think she's perfect too".

Before I could answer with exactly what I thought of her scheme, my phone started buzzing.

"Hello?"

On the other end of the line there was a bit of crackling and then "Hello, is this Hanna Standford?"

"Yeah, that's me. Who is this?"

I told you it was right. I thought I heard someone say on the other end of the line.

"Congratulations, Hanna. You've won a two weeks vacation in Priestley Woods." The voice was anything but enthusiastic. It sounded bored, and vaguely annoyed.

"Excuse me, could you repeat that?" I asked, while pushing the button to put the voice on speaker.

"Congratulations Hanna Stanford. You won a ticket to Priestley Woods Happy Camper experience."

More enthusiasm, Nerea. The voice was so faint that I thought I might be inventing it.

I looked at Lori with surprise.

She shrugged.

"There must be a mistake, I've never participated in any contest for this prize, you must have the wrong number"

"It's a unique experience you've won from buying..." There was a bit of a scuffle on the other end of the line "..tampons!"

"I mean I've certainly bought tampons, but wasn't there a code or something?"

"It was automatic" The voice appeared increasingly bored.

Lori snatched the phone from my hand "She doesn't believe your scams, ok? She won't fall for your lies. Bye" and then Lori hung up the phone. My phone.

"Excuse me!"

"You're too naïve, Hanna. Thank god you have me to protect you from fake advertisers and people trying to take advantage of you"

I didn't even think of it. Maybe Lori was right, they were probably going to ask for my credit card number next. "Thanks, Lori"

"No worries, babe. I got you." she winked and jumped up from the sofa. "I'm gunna get us popcorn and the Lip service DVD, since you had such a tragic date."

"You'd do that for me?" I asked, touched by the kindness. We had a monthly limit on how many times I could fan-girl over Frankie. I'd already reached mine three days ago, after the date with the 'my-cincilla-has-ocd-please-save-her' girl.

"Of course." Lori threw my phone in my direction just as it started buzzing.

"Hello?"

"Hello, this is Tampon for Lampo calling Hanna Stanford. I think there was a problem on the line. You officially won a vacation to Priestley-"

I hung up.

"Well, fool me once, shame on you. Fool me twice shame on me." I said, looking all smiley in Lori's direction.

But my friend had a look of utter shock painted on her face. "What have you done?"

"What do you mean?" I asked perplexed.

"Scammers don't call after you accused them of scamming!" She said. "I think it was a real prize. Check the number."

Unknown. "Shit," I said "Well, looks like there'll be no holiday prize"

There was hardly time to mourn the loss, though, when the phone buzzed yet again. This time, I pressed the green button under Lori's watchful eye.

"Hi Hanna" the person on the other end of the phone said. The voice was different and the tone sounded noticeably more rough. I was petrified. I'd heard the voice before, but I couldn't place it exactly, as if it came from an eerie dream I'd taken pains to forget.

"Yes, it's me," I said, as calmly as I could while my heart thundered inside my chest.

"You won a vacation to Priestley Wood at Happy Campers." The voice said sternly.

And this time I believed it.

Chapter 3
Artemis

"For Zeus' sake, what's got into you?" I asked.

Nerea, at the other end of the room, seemed oblivious to my irritation. Her hand was already snatching food from the banquet, the *cillphone* forgotten in her other hand.

"Are you trying to get us found out?" I insisted.

She pushed a fist full of blueberries into her mouth, "Of course not."

"Then what the hell is wrong with you?" I asked, approaching her.

A handful of lusciously ruby grapes disappeared into the black hole of her mouth.

I normally appreciated such appetite in my nymph but being ignored like this was intolerable. "Do you have any complaints, perhaps?" I asked with growing menace.

"How could I? You are the greatest Goddess to ever grace the top of the Olympus." She said with another mouthful of fruit distorting her voice.

Enough.

I stood between her and the food, leaning against the table. "Nerea!" I said, "Cut the stag shit and tell me the truth."

She gave me a gloomy look up and down "Why did you agree to this?" A little piece of grape was stuck at the side of her cheek, making the thin line of her mouth appear far from serious.

"I told you! I will be respected as a savage, powerful Goddess once more. I will get back my bow, and the woods, and all of us will finally be able to what we used to." I said making a gesture to point at the sheer obviousness of my reasoning.

Nerea's expression was unchanged.

"And really, when you hear what I've got in store for my sister-"

"-So, it has absolutely nothing to do with the fact that Callisto is involved?" She interrupted me.

I looked at her annoyed. "Why would I care about Callisto?"

Nerea was one of my most loyal nymphs, we had spent many restless hours together following animal tracks, we had ridden side-by-side for millennia through all types of terrain in the worst weather conditions. I could rely on her. She had even volunteered to help me hunt down Actaeon in order to indulge my wrath. All of this time and all of these experiences together and I had not yet seen her parade the disgruntled expression she wore in front of me right now "Uh-huh."

"Nerea, you don't really believe that I, the Great Goddess of the Hunt, might still have feelings for that nymph/woman/whatever she is..?"

"Uhh."

"Nerea, stop making noises and start talking, please. You're making an unpleasant situation worse and my temper is running thin."

Her gaze finally met mine, "I honestly think you are full of stag shit, Great Goddess of the Hunt. I know you. All of us who know you can see that Callisto holds a special place in your heart."

"Nerea, stop being absurd. Callisto is nothing to me but a lying cheater."

Nerea rolled her eyes and turned away from me once more. Her insolence would have not gone unpunished had she not been my only ally for the next two weeks, but as it was, ignoring her and dropping the topic seemed the wiser option.

Pity she didn't share the same objective.

"It is funny to me, my queen, that it's been over two thousand years and we are still at square one when it comes to her."

As usual, her bluntness broke through my shield of calm and I felt the old anger start to flare up once more.

"All you talk about is Callisto is a cheater here, Callisto is a cheater there. You seem deaf to what the sources say about her supposed betrayal. They say she did nothing wrong in fact-"

"NOTHING WRONG?" My hand closed around the edge of the table and I felt the wood crumble. "What do you mean *nothing wrong*?!" The noise of a storm thundered outside. "After what she did?!"

Nerea moved sideways and carefully selected a chicken wing. "Never mind" she said before taking a bite.

Oh, she wasn't going to get away with it that easily "how many times did I let her ride from Ephesus to Troy, hunting deer and stags next to me as if she was my queen rather than a Nymph? How many times? And then she had the audacity to -" I felt sorrow spring from my chest, replacing my anger. To my great shame, tears were burning behind my eyes. "And then she chose to -"

I couldn't finish. To Hades with tears.

With half a chicken wing still hanging from her mouth, Nerea offered me one of those pitying looks I hated. She swallowed. "Hush, my queen," she said. "It is too hard to remember." She put an arm around my shoulders.

"I can't believe it, Nerea. Remember when we met her? She was washing herself in the Ilisos, looking more radiant than any Goddess ever did..." I sounded pathetic to my own ears.

"I mean..your sister looks very radiant, I'd say-"

I shot her a warning look.

"Yes I remember, my queen." she corrected herself.

"And she looked so innocent. Remember? Callisto just looked at me and she said-"

"-If you are not a Goddess, my eyes are betraying me."

"Oh, you do remember?"

"How could I forget, my queen?" I knew there was sarcasm in her tone, and chose to ignore it. Nerea had been by my side through it all.

"Perhaps seeing her again and finally talking to her will give you what you need to move on," my nymph added.

I straightened my back and pushed her arm away.

"No Nerea. That's ridiculous. I plan on ignoring her."

"Sure, that seems mature," Nerea said, taking the last bite from the chicken wing. I shot her a look that forced her delicacy back into place "I am sure, my queen, that you'll find the best way to deal with such a difficult situation."

"There is no dealing. I wouldn't care for a human either way."

"As you say, my queen."

From the corner of my gaze, I saw Nerea rolling her eyes once more.

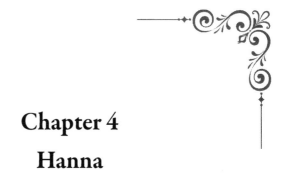

Chapter 4
Hanna

THE CAR TIPPED FROM side to side as I drove down the pebbled road.

Lori gave a big yawn and stretched her arms as high as the short car roof would allow. "Are we there, yet?" Her eyes remained stubbornly closed.

I turned around another bend in the road, and the campsite appeared, in all its woodland gLori, beyond the windscreen.

"Yes, here we are!" I said with renewed enthusiasm. The long hours sitting in my tiny Nissan had left me fighting a throbbing pain in my back and I could not wait to get out and stretch my legs.

The tents were arranged in a circular shape around the main campfire. On the northern edge of the circle stood what looked like the main tent, wide and tall enough to fit a small circus.

I approached the empty parking lot and turned off the engine. Even from inside the car cubicle, we could hear the sound of a river reverberating across the meadow. The grass seemed almost fake for how rich and green it looked waving in the light breeze.

I took a quick look at the clock: we'd made good time, not too late for tea. The sun was just dipping below the tree line, soon it would explode into a thousand shades of pink on the valley just behind. The thought of it made me smile as I leant back in my seat to take it all in.

If ever there was a paradise, this must be it.

"You promise that if it's too weird we can leave, right?" Lori asked, playing uneasily with her phone.

"Of course." I said, distracted by the view in front of me.

"It's that I still don't understand why they agreed to a two people vacation.. isn't it weird for a prize?"

"Lori, we've talked about it. A good thing happened and we are going to make the best of what this opportunity has to offer."

"I know, I know."

"So let's get out of our comfort zones, ok? Embrace nature. Look how beautiful it is!"

The bucolic landscape seemed to soothe Lori's worries. She took a deep breath. "Yes, you're right. Let's do this." She pushed the car's door open.

I savoured one more look at the view in front of me. Dad would have loved it: he always looked for scenic routes when we did our trips up north. We'd go for long hikes in the mountains together and he would point out all the different species of trees and birds we'd find...and bribe me with raspberries if I started to lag behind.

I pushed away the wave of nostalgia and stepped outside the car.

"Here you are!" A woman, tall and blonde, flung her arms wide open in our direction. She looked somewhere in her thirties and had the kind of skin I had thought could only be found in photoshopped beauty magazines.

I felt a stab of shame about the empty bags of crisps scattered on the front seat.

"Welcome to Priestley Wood All Women Retreat. My name is Eusachia" she said looking at us with the same enthusiasm kids reserve for Halloween treats.

"I thought it was called Happy Camper." Lori asked suspiciously.

The woman's smile grew impossibly wider "Well, it sure must be a happy camper who gets to spend two weeks at an all-women retreat, don't you think?" She winked at me.

Was it a wink of gay acknowledgement? I was painfully aware that I'd fail even the most sophisticated gaydar, so there was no way this woman just knew. And what were the options? Did the tampon company knew about my sexual history? No, that would be ridiculous. And alarming. I pushed the thought away.

"Let me help you unload your bags," Eusachia said. Before we could protest she had both of our bags, heavy enough to contain two weeks worth of clothes, loaded on her shoulders.

"I am sure you'll love these two weeks in Priestley Woods!" She threw another enthusiastic look at the two of us. "Let's settle you into your tents and then we can go for a tour, eh?"

"You said tents..as in, we're staying in multiple tents?" I asked.

"Yes, unfortunately there was a mistake in the booking and you ended up in different tents, but don't worry," Eusachia said, still appearing unbothered by the crushing weight on her shoulders "you won't be alone. You're both sharing with a fellow camper. It will help everyone break the ice!"

Sharing a tent with a stranger was not exactly how I had envisioned my holiday but I was determined to embrace it. I'd talked some big talk to Lori about wanting to get out of my comfort zone and meet new people, so there was no going back now.

For her part, Lori seemed to have regained her enthusiasm in the short time she'd been relieved of luggage duty.

"Here we are!" Eusachia deposited the bags in front of each of our tents, side by side, and stood back to let us explore.

The tents were identical: two thin mattresses, two sleeping bags, a portable stove and a few other essential objects near the doorway. All very well kept. New, almost.

"Thank you," I said.

"Not at all, it's a pleasure!" She said, waving a hand dismissively in my general direction. "Ready to meet the rest of the campers?"

We both nodded and rushed to stash our bags before Eusachia hurried us off across the meadow behind our tents.

"Very well, then. Let's get you both to the Chow Hall. That's where we eat and play and hang out. If you ever just want to chat or play cards or, I don't know, maybe drink a couple of beers, you want to head to the main tent. That's where it all happens. Breakfast is served there from 7 to 9, Lunch 12 to 1:30 and dinner runs from 7 to 8:30."

Eusachia had barely drawn breath. I snuck a look at Lori as we got closer to the main tent. She looked back at me, wide-eyed. We were practically running.

"And ta-daaa" Eusachia said, crossing the threshold and throwing her arms out wide again. "Welcome to the Chow Hall"

Twenty pairs of eyes turned to stare at us at once.

The woman closest to us a brunette with simple clothes and and an unenthusiastic smile, came to offer her hand. "Hello. My name is Nerea, I'm the lead yoga teacher, here." Her voice, low and even, sounded familiar. I studied her face, we definitely hadn't met before.

I shook her hand "It's a pleasure. Are you about to start a lesson?" I said, throwing nervous glances at the many strangers who were still staring at us.

"Yes," she replied curtly. "Feel free to join."

With that, the yoga teacher offered us a small bow and turned to address the class.

"That's great! I am so glad you met Nerea" Eusachia lowered her voice and leaned in towards us "She is a bit weird, but mostly well meaning."

I smiled politely.

'Here we have out banquet table' she said, as she drove us deeper into the tent, 'There are refreshments available all day long. And yes, I am talking the alcoholic type.' Eusachia winked and nudged me in the ribs with such powerful enthusiasm, I suspected I would deal with a bruise in the morning.

"...Neither of us can handle alcohol well ,unfortunately." I said, in my best sorrowful impression.

"What a pity! Oh dear. Well, will find some other trick to help you relax"

Lori leaned in my ears "..is she talking about drugs?!"

"Shh"

"And here, finally, is where we do diy classes. Painting. Dried Flower Composition. Crochet. All very lovely alternatives."

In the circle of chair Eusachia was pointing, sat a woman alone. She was chipping at the piece of wood in her lap with the concentration of an artist in a creative rapture. She was leaning forward and an unruly strand of chocolate hair covered her eyes, like a rebellious soldier deserting a ruffled war. The muscles of her forearm rippled under her inked skin with every stroke of her hand.

She did not raise her eyes to meet us. Which was lucky, because she would have caught me staring at her with the same ridiculous expression I reserved for surprise birthday parties and attractive women who left me tongue tied.

She was -well, my type. The type I had sworn to stay away from. I followed her fingers as they brushed the chips of wood off her thigh and my stomach took a dive past my belt as I willed a deity above to please prevent me from doing anything embarassing.

As if on cue her eyes raised to mine.

There was anger hidden in them, and something else- acknowledgement, desire. Sadness? The bottom half of my body felt paralyzed as her expression turned more furious, and the glint in her eyes flared with the strength of a fire.

From a place far far away came Eusachia's voice '... It's group therapy day on saturday. Some need it more than others.'

Lori's right elbow hit me in the ribs. Another bruise. "Hey, Earth to Hanna."

I turned towards her, still in a daze, and quickly tried to compose my face.

"I know what you are looking at, and that's a no." She whispered in my ear.

"I don't know what you are talking about." I replied, feigning innocence.

"That woman you were just ogling over there looks like the quintessential definition of a bad girl and you are going to stay away from her. I'm holding you to your own promise, remember?"

"You're right, I'm being weak." I threw a last glance at the criminally hot stranger and sat down next to Eusachia, who had decided we were in need of tea.

With a bit of luck the mysterious woman was going to leave tomorrow, and I could label this strange lure I felt towards her as the result of a too-long dry spell.

I threw a glance- just a little glance- at the woman in the back again, but she had disappeared. I ignored the spark of disappointment threatening to catch fire inside me.

"Don't you find it all a bit weird?" Lori asked as we left our empty cups on the bar and walked back on the the luscious grass. The sun was now almost completely set on the horizon.

My whole body felt awakened, pulsing with energy. And I wasn't sure I could blame it on the mega-indulgent chocolate cake we'd just shared. "What do you mean?"

"The names: Eusachia, Sarisi.. Don't they seem.. original to you?"

"A bit." I said, shrugging my shoulders.

"And the free vacation.. I don't know.. something feels sketchy."

"Oh c'mon, we have barely met anyone!" I threw a look at my friend, who was still chewing on her bottom lip. "Ok, fine, what's your theory then?"

"We're being recruited into a cult."

"Lori." I stopped in my tracks and turned towards her. "This is not a cult." The thin lines on Lori's face did not smooth out. "Tell you what. If a cult wants to recruit us, they'll have to try harder than a camping retreat."

"Like what?"

"Unlimited supply of crisps, of course," I said with a smirk. Finally, Lori's frown was replaced by a short laugh.

With the crisp evening air flowing through my curls and the magnificent sight of twilight shattering the blue sky in an array of pinks on the horizon, I smiled back at my friend.

"It's going to be fine, Lori."

She nodded. "Ok, fine. I believe you."

We said goodnight in front of the entrance of my tent and I crouched to cross the dark threshold. A long, deep shiver ran down my spine. The temperature seemed to have suddenly dropped despite the heavy material covering the sleeping space. I pulled my sweater closer to my body as my breath drew smokey puffs in front of me.

My eyes, still adjusting to the dim light, fell on the figure dragging a bag across the small floorspace.

My stomach dropped.

Oh...

Oh sheep. My two weeks vacation had just suddenly taken a very interesting turn.

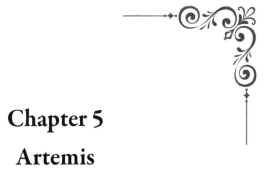

Chapter 5
Artemis

NO. NONONO.

Fair enough that I was trapped for two weeks on a ridiculous camping trip. Not to mention Nerea teaching *yogie-* or whatever those weird balancing movements were called.

And sure, I hardly expected Aphrodite to just wait for Callisto/Hanna/whoever she was and I to meet spontaneously or - even better - at my own discretion.

But was it truly necessary to have Callisto and I share a tent together?

Of course it was, knowing my sister.

Callisto's ambrosia eyes were piercing through me with the same ruthless focus of a hunter drawing in on her prey. A new wave of fear bubbled inside my stomach.

Before she could say anything, before I could even let my human version of an ex breath out, I abandoned the bag and fled the tent.

At the Chow Hall I found Nerea absorbed in chatting with one of Aphrodite's ladies.

"Seriously?!" I asked indignantly. "You couldn't have tried to avoid the couple tenting? Whose side are you on, Nerea?".

"I had to make a compromise" Nerea said noncommittally.

I looked at her terrified "What in Hades did you exchange it for?"

She stretched her arms high up into the air "Your sister insisted you be the meditation teacher. I thought we'd get found. We're already off of a weird start."

Eusachia's was leaning on the banquet table, slurping loudly the last drops of tea. "If you growled less, perhaps she wouldn't have had to exchange that, don't you think?"

I ignored her. "Why didn't you warn me then, Nerea?"

"You don't take bad news well, my queen."

"You should have done it anyway!"

Nerea shrugged.

"Once I am back on the Olympus you'll pay for this.."

"That might not happen for a long while.." Eusachia chimed from behind her comically tiny teacup. Her annoying smirk betrayed just how much she was enjoying this.

I shot her a murderous look.

Nerea kept stretching, impervious to my anger.

"So what am I supposed to do now?"

"As you said, ignore her. Go to sleep." Nerea stretched her hips in a downward position, offering me a full view of her backside.

"It's not even seven o'clock."

"Perhaps you could just try talking to her. After all you are fully over her, aren't you? And she has no idea who you are. So you can start fresh," Eusachia said. Apparently she was oblivious as her queen about when it was time to shut up.

That nymph was going to pay too, Goddess' word. I just had to wait until Aphrodite got distracted.

I paced the tent in anger. An idea crossed my mind. "Very well then" I clenched my jaw "I want to change: bring me Euphebe, instead of Nerea, she'll know how to be of help."

"First," Aphrodite's lady said, "there are no take-backsies and you already made your choice about which nymph would be the one to help you. Second," she took a step towards me, "Nerea was the only one of your nymphs actually willing to support you with this."

"That's not true," I said in shock. "Nerea, tell her that's not true."

Nerea shut her eyes and we both watched her chest rose and fell. "Of course not, Great Goddess of the Hunt, any of us nymphs would be happy to serve you in any and all circumstances." She'd barely bothered to complete this reassurance when she gripped her hips and turned her torso sideways.

I stormed out of the tent in blind rage. How could Nerea do this to me? How dare they turn against me? I may not have my full powers here, due to the stupid agreement with Aphrodite, but they must know that crossing a Goddess was a huge risk. *Wait until I get back on Olympus,* I thought.

I will make them all pay for this.

I walked back to the tent dreading every step that took me closer to her. I had considered all of the alternatives: running and hiding until the end of two weeks, begging my sister to allow me back in the Olympus, admitting defeat and spend a lifetime as a human. Everything, absolutely everything seemed preferable to facing Callisto's eyes again, but this was worse still: I was doomed to spend night after night laying next to her look-alike.

I paused in front of the moss green tent. A savage Goddess would face a human. A thousand humans, even. A million, without any fear at all.

And now Callisto was just a tiny, weak, mortal creature that could do nothing against me. She could not kill me, nor ruin me, nor hurt me. I was in control. And she was not my ex.

I crossed the threshold and found myself eye to eye with Callisto's perplexed face.

I returned the look with cold disdain.

"I don't bite, you know," Callisto said.

The audacity. The audacity she had to talk to me after what she'd done.

"But I do." I retorted.

I saw Hanna/Callisto lowering her eyes to the ground as if embarrassed. Oh! She thought I meant... as if I was actually interested in being around her, as if I could ever lay my mouth on her soft skin again. As if it didn't still pain me to reminisce about the time we lay asleep under the stars, hiding at the bottom of Olympus' caves to avoid any indiscrete eyes. It was the day she told me she loved me and wished to reign at my side. Human Callisto smelled exactly like then, when she'd looked at me with glittering eyes, curled up in my arms.

"You mean...as in-? Human Callisto said, waking me up from the daydream.

Could she read my thoughts?

My skin felt hot, as if her proximity alone was searing through me "I don't like company" I growled back.

"Someone must have woken up on the wrong side of the tent.." human Callisto said.

I met her eyes and a new wave of anger swelled inside me. *Leave me alone*, I wanted to bark in her direction. *You were the death of me.*

"If you want either of us to be transferred to a new tent, you'll have to talk to the director, I'm just glad to be in here for free," Hanna said without breaking a sweat.

"I'm just going to go to sleep."

"It's not even 7:30" Callisto replied, surprised.

I did not answer. I just turned around and pretended her eyes, her voice, her smell were part of a bitter sweet dream. Just another of many I'd had since she'd left.

Chapter 6
Hanna

"WHAT A MONUMENTAL JERK. Can you imagine?"

The rich food we were served for dinner had done very little to soothe my roommate-induced bad mood.

"I did notice her giving you the side eyes a couple of times earlier, but I assumed she was just an angry personality" Lori gripped my arm.

"It was so uncalled for."

She paused "Are you sure you've never met her?"

"Don't you think I would have remembered?" Especially those arms. I would have remembered those arms.

"Perhaps in one of those secret sexual rampages you went on in college when I wasn't looking?"

"Lori, for the thousandth time, there were no sexual rampages. I was in the library. Studying."

"Fine. Fine" Lori raised her hand in the air as if to surrender. "... but are you sure that's it?"

"What do you mean?"

"You are not the type to get so worked up over someone's behavior. I can count on... one finger of one hand when you actually got mad at someone.."

I had met plenty of rude pet owners in my time at the clinic. Lori had a point. Something about that woman was getting on my nerves in a way no one else ever had. Perhaps it was the fact that, just a few hours earlier, I had been excited at the prospect of sharing a room with Ms Broody Butch. Maybe that's what was getting to me: the wastefulness of it all. I mean, it was hard to look at her skilled hands and not let my mind wander to the exquisite power they could produce if they were employed in a gratifying manner.

That, though, I'd rather not share with Lori.

"She was incredibly rude. And I have to share a tent with her for two weeks. You'd be pretty worked up too!"

Lori gave me a thorough look but made no further comment on the topic. Instead, she offered a reassuring smile "If you'd feel more comfortable you can sleep in my tent. The lady I am sharing with, Loelia, seems pretty friendly."

"No," I said, clenching my fist "I'm not going to run away like a child. If she has a problem with me then she can be the one to leave."

"That's my fierce baby Hanna" Lori said with a smirk and a pat on my back.

Like a talisman, I repeated Lori's words as I reached the tent's entrance. I took a deep breath and stepped in as quietly as possible.

My roommate's anger still resonated across the pitch black of the tent, like the echo of an old scream. How can someone who's never met me be so mad at the prospect of spending time in my proximity? We were strangers. She shouldn't care. I shouldn't care.

But as I slipped into the sleeping bag as quietly I could, and undressed in the tiny confinement it offered, I felt my fake bravado dripping away. I shivered from the cold air and reached for my pyjamas. The family of bears printed on the front did not help with my new embarrassment.

I shot one last glance at the figure sleeping on the other side of the tent. Her back was still facing me but the attraction I felt towards her, like heavy chords between the two of us, inching me closer, was just as powerful as before. Even in pitch darkness, I could have drawn the shape of her body in her sleeping bag.

I drifted asleep with these thoughts swimming through my mind.

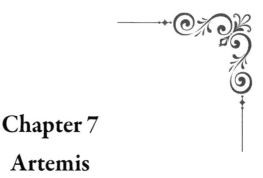

Chapter 7
Artemis

CALLISTO'S FIRST SNORE filled the tent. The noise was soft and peaceful. She was probably dreaming of unicorns and cheese - or whatever humans dreamed about when Orpheus breathed on them.

Each rise and fall of her chest, steady and rhythmic, was like a kick in the stomach.

How did Callisto ended up being the unfazed one? How did she end up tormenting me even here, in the sanctuary of the woods, my home?

It was unbearable.

I dashed out of the tent before I could allow anymore of her to get to me. I covered the distance between the edge of the meadow and the end of the campsite in quick strides. The cold night air awakened my senses and the vegetation on the border of the campsite shook under it, welcoming me into its safety.

The power of the barrier enclosing the camp was so powerful that I felt its energy before I saw it. For several hours the previous day I had tried to find a hole in the fabric of my sister's spell, with no luck. Aphrodite had effectively trapped me in here.

The sound of approaching footstep caught my attention. They were clumsy. None of my nymphs would ever be louder than a breeze.

I clenched my jaw. "You shouldn't be here."

"My queen"

"I am not your queen." I said, staring beyond the transparent barrier. "If my sister were to hear you calling me this, she'd off your head."

I was only mildly concerned about it.

Loelia's auburn hair was falling over her shoulder in a shiny cascade of moonlit silk. Her dark eyes were studying my expression "You couldn't handle that" she said. She slid behind me, her hand resting on my shoulder.

"Oh, I could" I replied.

She giggled stupidly, as if I had made a funny joke. Her touch was unwelcome. It had been for a long time, but Aphrodite's nymphs were as strong headed as my sister and naturally unflinching in front of rejection. "You don't have to be tough with me," she said, ignoring my words. "I've seen you vulnerable."

Her other hand came to rest on the back on my neck. My skin tingled where her warm fingertips drew delicate lines. It was reassuring, it was familiar.

Tonight, I hated it. "Loelia, stop."

"As you wish, my queen." She retracted her hand.

"I told you not to call me that."

"You know my loyalty is to you, Goddess of The Hunt."

Nobody called me that anymore. Well, only Nerea when she wanted to tease me. Nobody feared me anymore: neither my own nymphs, nor the other Gods. To all of them, I was just a pathetic mess of a divinity, who had fallen for a nymph and got betrayed as a result. I was the cautionary tale about the importance of sticking to your own kind.

"Why?" I asked.

Loelia looked at me confused.

"Why are you here?"

"I know this is hard for you and I wanted to help," she said.

"Then tell me why is my sister doing this to me? Wasn't the centaur blind date enough?"

"I don't know" Loelia said, sitting on a heavy branch next to me. Her hand grazed my leg. "It really is cruel. But, you know, you don't have to play the game her way, my queen."

I looked at her, so surprised by her implication that I forgot to scold her for using that title again. I had thought of nothing other than how to escape the situation since I caught a glimpse of Callisto in the Chow Hall earlier in the day. I thought I had considered all of my options: that is, I had none.

"You could just keep away from the human and find another outlet for your...frustration" her eyes glinted with mischief. "I offer myself as a volunteer."

There had been times when I would have taken such an offer. But now my brain was filled with the image of Callisto sleeping peacefully in the tent - our tent - and I was stuck.

"I wish she could just disappear."

"Your sister?"

"No, Callisto. I wish she could just go back to wherever she came from," I scuffed the cool earth with my shoes, immediately regretting how pathetic that line must have sounded.

My shoulders fell and my head tipped forward, escaping Loelia's gaze. I wanted to forget her presence and the judgement they all quietly imposed on me. Because then maybe, this wretched state of mine and this pain I felt, would cease to exist with no witnesses to bare the memory. I couldn't handle pity.

When our eyes met, though, I saw tenderness in her look, "Why do you hold on to the past so tight?" She asked, there was softness in her voice, too. I must really look a mess.

Shame washed over me again, "You wouldn't understand."

"My queen is the Goddess of Love.. as you reminded me just a minute ago"

I sat down and took a deep breath. "She was different."

Loelia offered an encouraging smile "How?"

"She was generous and naive, and...really funny, she always surprised me that way. She was a phenomenal archer too -and you know it takes a lot to impress me- but she could really hit any target. We never caught a damn prey with her, though, and I suspected it was on purpose. She didn't like violence, her heart was too soft...she was the kind of person everyone naturally came to love.. She always asked too many questions and at the wrong time and her laugh was so powerful, whenever we were out, she always ended up scaring away any animals for miles around us. There was this one time we were camping by the river Acheloos..-"

My voice trailed off at the memory.

"-Why do you do this to yourself? It's like you enjoy hurting" Loelia said. She shook her head slowly and leaned towards me.

"I don't" I said quietly, more to myself, than her.

"Don't you remember? She cheated on you. Had she really been this lovely, would she have done that-?"

The irritation I felt at my sister's maid, bubbled up into anger.

".. in the end, my queen, even if it's hard to see it, Callisto was just -"

"Don't-"

"... a cheating cow"

My brain short-circuited into a furious explosion "Leave."

Loelia's face contorted into an expression halfway between surprised and terrified "Goddess, but I am on your side" she tried to reach for my arm "what she did was beyond forgivable. You've said it yourself countless times! I don't understand what-"

The sound of distant thunder reached us from beyond the barrier. I fixed my stare beyond the glass-like wall "I told you to leave."

"I'm sorry. I am very sorry. I only came here to make you feel better" she said, her hand stroked my neck again.

I grabbed it with enough strength to crush a human bone and pulled her close enough she could no longer mistake my words. "You are just as selfish as your queen. You take what you want under a thin layer of self serving generosity."

"But-'"

My expression quieted her. "Leave or I'll make you"

I released her arm and she retreated a couple of steps.

"Nobody can compete with a ghost" she said, in a sad tone.

"Nobody is asking you to."

She seemed to hold her breath for a second, before the sound of her clumsy steps died down.

I stood quiet for what felt like hours staring at a tiny snail cross the barrier unscathed. Snails could get past Aphrodite's tricks, but I couldn't.

Jealous of a snail. Oh, the irony.

"Perhaps we can make a home for it?" Came Callisto's voice from the dark recess of an everyday memory.

"It's a snail. Let him make his own house"

"What if it's a she? You wouldn't leave her homeless, would you?"

To Hades with the damn snail.

Chapter 8
Hanna

I THREW A GLANCE TO my left but I knew it was unnecessary: I could tell my roommate was not here. It's like the presence of her had dissolved as I slept.

I distracted myself by getting dressed hurriedly and stepped out of the tent into an unusually bright day: not a cloud could be seen anywhere and the little dew drops under my feet were surprisingly pleasant.

Nobody could let one impolite jerk ruin such a day.

I set off to look for Lori, who I was sure was having a very different experience with the dew. I happened to know that she'd forgotten the 'camping flip flops' back on my bag. I still didn't understand why she called my old woolen slippers that, but if wearing them meant she felt more comfortable in nature, I was prepared to cheer her on as she roamed around the campsite in fluffy blue footwear.

When I reached the main tent, handfuls of women were scattered all over and Lori, at the far edge of it, was fishing granola from her milk bowl "So? Had a good night?"

I cracked the back of my neck and look at her through a sleepy smile. "I've had better ones, but it was fine I guess."

"So no trouble," she said, relieved. "Good-"

"Did I hear trouble?" Eusachia said enthusiastically, appearing out of nowhere. "I hope everyone is enjoying their accommodation" she said with a smile that would have blinded a toothpaste ad actress.

"Yep, no p-"

"-Actually my friend is struggling with her roommate" Lori interrupted before I could finish pretending everything was perfectly fine, thank you very much. She was holding the cup as if ready to swing it in my defence.

"Oh nooo" Eusachia said with an exaggerated frown.

"Yes. Very difficult personality. Hard to imagine why she'd sign up for a happy camper experience if sulking is such a favourite activity of hers" Lori said.

"I am so sorry to hear that."

"Is there a chance perhaps we could exchange tents and be assigned together?" Lori said hopeful.

I appreciated her gesture, but I didn't want to be rescued.

Eusachia's doe eyes were wrinkled with sorrow "Unfortunately, it's complicated-"

"There is no need. I am perfectly fine. Really-" I tried to interject.

"-Why is it a problem?" Lori insisted "I asked my roommate and, for some reason, she seemed more than happy to exchange."

For some reason! Really, it was like Lori was missing eyes.

Eusachia's gaze darted between the two of us before landing on me "You're paired with Artemis, aren't you?"

Artemis. It was a very fitting name.

"I'm not sure-"

"You are." Eusachia held eye contact with me with the force of a StrongMan competitor.

Artemis. When did I heard that name before? Maybe a school friend?

"See, Hanna," Eusachia leaned over and grabbed my hand, vaulting the line between campsite organizer and camping attendees. "Artemis is going through a very rough time.."

"Really?"

Eusachia gestured at me to lean closer. "She's had a very rough break-up, somewhat recently" she said "And she's not fully over it, yet. Don't ask about it, mind. She gets pissy."

With that revelation she leaned back on the chair and sighed loudly.

A wave of understanding washed over me. I knew first hand the struggles of a wounded heart, and there was nothing like it to bring out the very worst from a person.

Lori, next to me, had the air of a teacher listening to a pupil describing how their dog has eaten their homework. "Just because you're hurting, it doesn't give you the right to act like a prick," she said. "You're right, of course," Eusachia said, nodding vehemently. "But given the circumstances, perhaps kindness might soften her up faster than a more.. argumentative approach."

"If she can be softened up" I said, still doubtful. The woman didn't strike me as a helpless kitten in need of a cuddle, more like a savage lioness looking to draw blood.

Eusachia paused and turned towards me. Her obsidian eyes were fixed so intently on my brown ones that it seemed as if she was trying to mine an answer from them.

"She just needs to feel safe," she said, with a sad smile "That's all the tough-looking ones need."

She blinked. And before I could reply her overenthusiastic smile was back "So ready for today's challenge?"

Lori looked at me, alarmed.

"What kind of challenge, exactly?" I asked, trying to push away the image of Artemis purring.

"Archery, of course!"

I poured a generous dose of coffee into one of the cups between us. *"All you need is Love -just call Cupid!"* was the odd inspirational quote printed on the side.

"Just like the Hunger Games.." Lori said with some cautious optimism colouring her voice.

"What?"

"The movie where there are districts and everyone is poor and then Katniss tries to save her sister and..."

Lori's voice faded into the background. Artemis was back.

She crossed the threshold with her unmistakable swagger and the yoga teacher by her side. I watched, struck by what an odd pair they looked, as they sat at the table closest to the entrance. Trusting she would not look our way, I searched Artemis' features, studying the curve of her cheekbones and the slope of her lips. I imagined drawing my fingers across them *Who has turned your mouth into a thin line*? I'd ask. *How did they set your eyes on fire?*

I imagined the chocolate eyes flashing while looking in mine. With desire, not anger, for once.

"...And then they overthrow the government but she hates them because they've killed her sister."

Eusachia smiled politely "Sounds unmissable." She turned towards me, "looking forward to seeing the two of you throw some arrows around."

It took me a second to regain my wits "I wouldn't miss it" I said, feeling much less certain than I sounded.

There was something about Eusachia that was mildly intimidating but I couldn't quite put my finger on it. As she blinded me with another of those pearly white smiles of her, I had a vivid picture of her sending an arrow through someone's throat. *What a weird image*, I thought. All the fresh air must have been getting to me.

"We are Katnissing today!" Lori said with unaffected glee.

I smiled back "Prepare to be impressed," I said.

I threw a new, hopeful glance, in the direction of Artemis. Perhaps I had not given her a fair chance.

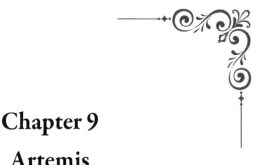

Chapter 9
Artemis

"HOLY MOLY" THE HIGH-pitched scream broke the summer haze in the meadow, suspending the performance of a band of crickets playing nearby. "How the hell did you do that!?"

The bow hung limp in human Callisto's hand but her eyes were still fixed on the target ahead. An arrow stood perfectly centred against the white and black circles.

"I.. I'm not sure..must be a serious case of beginner's luck." Her eyes kept darting back and forth from her hands to the hypnotic target ahead.

"This is brilliant, Hanna!" Eusachia said, clapping her hands enthusiastically. Behind her the uproar of cute little "ohhh"s and "ahh"s from the gathered nymphs reminded me of a flock of geese.

What a charade.

I rolled my fist into a tight ball and turned my eyes away from the spectacle. Archery was just another of Nerea and Aphrodite conjoined surprises, this time, though, I was being forced to witness the triumphant achievement of my ex's look alike. What a great way to spend the morning.

"Perhaps we could start a challenge between you and our champion" Eusachia said, turning towards me.

Oh no, she didn't really mean...

"Artemis, dear, why don't you try to defend your title?" she asked, with a summoning hand gesture.

Try? Try to defend. What a damn- Enough was enough.

"I'm happy to give a live demonstration," I said. Eusachia was standing nearby, her mouth bent into a knowing smirk that was grating on my nerves. I certainly didn't need any further invitation. I raised the cheap wooden bow Nerea had obtained for me. My attention was caught by the vein in Eusachia's neck as it pulsed against her pale skin in a way that seemed to invite my arrow right into it. "Even better, perhaps a moving, living target might be the most suitable." I said, relishing the image of my sister's maid finally quiet.

Eusachia face darkened.

"I'm a vegetarian," Callisto said, misunderstanding my intentions. She stepped in front of my bow with her hand outstretched, "and really I am happy for you to keep the title. I was just lucky."

Of course she was a damn vegetarian.

I lowered the bow "Are you afraid?" I said, ignoring her hand and throwing a threatening glance at Eusachia.

"Excuse me?" Callisto asked.

I brought my eyes back to her familiar features. Callisto's indignant expression made for such a stark contrast to her usual springy, friendly attitude that she almost looked like a different person. "I asked you if you're afraid," I said louder. I swallowed, I had been trying hard to keep my tone level.

Her hazelnut eyes stared squarely back at me, her determination growing in front of my eyes. She bit her lips. "Not of you."

"Good to know," I wasn't afraid of her either. Not at all.

"Very well then, I guess this challenge is exactly what we need to settle the matter."

"Hanna, do you think this is a good idea?" Her human friend hissed in her direction. "I mean, she has a *weapon*."

"How many rounds?" human Callisto asked.

The entire group of nymphs had gone quiet.

"Three." I said.

"Fine."

She took a deep breath and looked at the arrow she had just shot, again. It was as if I could hear the peptalk happening in her head.

"Do you really think you can beat me?" I asked to spare her the humiliation "if you want you can bow out, and I'll be gracious about it."

Her eyes burned in mine "Watch me." And I did watch as she stormed towards Eusachia and extended her hand for one of the arrows the nymph held.

"Please can I have one of those?"

Eusachia only hesitated for a second. Then she handed Callisto the arrow.

"I'll start." It wasn't a question: without waiting for any encouragement, Callisto drew the bow in one fluid motion. One deep breath, and her shoulders relaxed. I watched carefully as she took aim to a nearby target, her expression laser focused on the tiny circle in the centre.

One, two...Three.

And then she shot.

The arrow flew across the field. It drew a perfect arch in the sky and squarely hit the tiny white circle.

Everyone was quiet.

"Are we still calling it beginner's luck?" Her friend asked with a nervous giggle.

I turned toward Callisto. Tiny pearls of sweat were beading her forehead and the breeze was playing with her hair, bouncing her unruly locks around her shoulders. She lowered the bow and a ray of light cast a beam behind her. At once I saw it: she was Callisto. My Callisto.

"Everyone stop staring and just...go back to shooting things!" I yelled . The rest of the nymphs got back to their places. Even Eusachia Only Nerea remained where she stood, her gaze fixed on Callisto.

The corner of Callisto's mouth twitched. "Your turn."

I only allowed myself one last glance at her before turned to aim my shot at Callisto's target. The arrow she had sent was still there, perfectly centred. I knew what I had to do. Nerea, Eusachia and all of Aphrodite's vapid maids would see exactly who they were playing against. And Callisto, of course. Especially her.

I drew the bow, holding my elbow at shoulder's height.

"You know I am unbeatable, right?"

"So am I." Callisto winked.

"You'll have to prove that"

"Any time, my queen" she said, bending in a over-the-top bow. Her hands were holding the hem of her dress and her bare feet were peeking out, covered in leaves.

I pulled her closer, my arm around her waist, reaching for the place behind her ear that would cause her breath to hitch."I am your love, not your queen."

"That won't get you any bonus points when I beat you at archery...my love" she said, kissing the top of my nose.

"It's cute that you think you can beat a Goddess"

"It's cute that you still so dramatically underestimate your nymph"

I blinked and felt the string release from my hand.

The arrow flew across the meadow. It tipped up and then fell in a great downward arc towards the circles just below. It was less than a couple of feet away from the target, when I turned my eyes away. I had just learned what all of the nymphs had already guessed: it was a bad shot. The arrow landed a little to the right of Callisto's. I had missed the target by no more than a couple of fingers.

It could have been miles, for all the good it did.

To Hades with damn memories.

Callisto was determined to ruin my existence, even from the depths of my own brain.

"That was great!" Loelia chimed in, uninvited.

"That was stagshit," I thundered in response.

The crickets in the background were the only sound in the meadow.

Eusachia, at last, seemed to revive."Good thing you have two more tries" she said, apparently nervous. She moved to offer me an arrow.

"No need." I said. "I concede the victory."

"What?!" Nerea's shock was mirrored in the eyes of the rest of the nymphs.

"You heard me, I concede the victory to my opponent."

I let the bow fall to my feet. I looked at my arrow, stuck neatly next to Callisto's one, taunting me. I had to leave.

When I turned, I met my old favourite eyes, caramel and round with surprise, glistening under the unrepentant sun.

She was right in front of me, obstructing my passage.

"You can't just concede victory" Callisto argued.

"I just did" I said, looking away from her, feeling my heartbeat accelerating.

Her hands flew to her waist and she bit her lips "That would make *my* victory meaningless."

"That sounds like not my problem, doesn't it? I've already granted it to you."

Without waiting to see her eyes turn from surprise to anger as she processed what I'd just said, I turned, as dignified as I could, and walked in the direction of the tent.

Chapter 10

Hanna

THREE DAYS AFTER THE archery competition, I shot up, wide awake, startled by the sound of a piercing cry ripping through the quiet of the night.

I looked around while my heart thundered in my chest.

Artemis was in the tent. That was new; I had not seen her since she had left me pissed off with a bow in my hand and a champion title I had not earned.

"Did you hear that?" I asked, out of instinct more than any particular desire to talk to her.

The blade in her hand answered my question. She was fully dressed and if she had been sleeping, any trace of it was already wiped off her features. Her hair were so perfectly ruffled the strands seemed to have been arranged by a movie hair crew.

My mind was gaining lucidity. The familiar shot of adrenaline was jolting my instincts awake. "What do you plan on doing with that, exactly?" I said nodding at the knife in her hand.

"Whatever the threat, there is nothing a quality bow can't solve, or, alternatively, a knife," she whispered in my direction.

"So you're one of those people who watch too many action movies, huh?' I said, grabbing the torch and the first aid kit.

Another scream burst through the fabric of the tent.

53

I made to leave but she moved to obstruct my way. We josselled for a few seconds, me trying to side step her and her shepherding me back to place. Frustrated, I stopped and found myself face to face with her collarbone. Actually, lower, but with someone's life apparently in danger, it felt tactless to indulge in the visual appreciation.

"You're not going anywhere" Artemis said, looking at me as if I had lost my mind. "I'm going outside and you're staying put."

"Oh really?" I said

"Yes. Really."

I made my move while she paused, darting around her and outside before she could offer another of her uninvited orders.

She was at my side, before I had even had a chance to blink, "I told you it is not safe out here. Go back."

I turned to face her, hoping my irritation and adrenaline boost made up for our height difference and made me more intimidating. I put as much authority into my words as possible, "Look, what I do, I decide. What you do, feel free to take initiative. Understood?"

Artemis seemed too stunned to reply.

Without wasting time to see if she would find her tongue, my eyes scanned the nearby tent. I had to make sure Lori was safe.

"She's fine" Artemis informed me, as if reading my thoughts.

"How do you know?"

"I can hear her snoring from here."

"You must have a supersonic ear then, because my friend does not snore."

"I can only tell you what I hear," she replied shrugging.

"And I don't trust you."

I peeked through the flap of the tent and found Lori snoring softly. She was safe. I relaxed my shoulders, ignoring the fact that Artemis actually did seem to know something more than I did about my long term roommate.

"That direction" Artemis said from my side.

Several of the other women stood in their night gowns near their tents, lighting the way like a swarm of fireflies.

"Again, how exactly do you anticipate using that?" I said nodding at the knife as we rushed towards the screams.

"It's either a human threat or an animal threat, so either way I plan to aim and kill."

"What?!?" I stopped and flung out my arm to catch hers and wheel her around to face me once again. I tried hard to ignore the flex of her bicep under my fingers. She could easily resist me but she didn't. "We are not going to kill a human or an animal. No matter what. Do you understand?"

"I thought we had a rule of "what I do, I decide. What you do, feel free to take initiative." Did I get it right?" She said with a cocked eyebrow and a hard glare that were equally attractive and irritating.

"Not that much initiative." I said stone-faced. I wasn't backing down.

A third scream pierced the breezy night air. This time, I was also certain it came from the woods.

I quickened my steps. "Follow *my* lead. And for goodness' sake don't throw that knife at anyone or anything."

Artemis furrowed brow and darkened expression suited her: a stunning queen of darkness about to eat someone's heart. "May I ask who gave you the title of leader?"

"Well let's see, first, I'm a vet. Second, I hold a Wildlife Animal Behavior Level 3 certification, and last, considering how graciously I handled your behaviour over the past few days, I'd say my talents for handling difficult animals extended to humans just as well."

Artemis opened her mouth to say something, paused, and closed it again. We walked hurried and silent through the first line of trees.

"I let you have the victory..." she said, as we waded further into the woods.

"That was mine anyway, I literally I won it."

Then we both saw him: a majestic red deer, with meters long horns crowning his head. I had never seen such a beautiful specimen. Five meters ahead, stood petrified Loelia, my friend's roommate. She must have been the one screaming but judging by the deer's dark eyes, darting between the three of us, he must have been just as frightened.

I threw a look at Artemis, still firmly gripping her damned knife. Her gaze was focused on the animal, the muscles in her hand twitching from the pressure.

I approached her sideways, making sure to walk slowly and gently so as to not spook the wild creature.

"Here" I said low and monotone, bowing my head.

The moon was blinking unhelpfully at the blade in Artemis' hand and it was just a matter of time before the deer would catch sight of it. From there it could go either way.

Let the damn knife go.

The blade in her hand was just an outstretched arm away, so I had to try.

With my eyes still fixed on the deer and the sound of my own heartbeat drowning out any other, I grabbed Artemis' wrist and slid my fingers down slowly. My breath hitched when my fingers came in contact with her skin and a shiver rolled between our hands. She flinched but did not fight my grip.

The knife handle was just beneath my palm but Artemis's hold gave no sign of relenting.

I gave a little squeeze of encouragement.

"Please." I said it so low, I doubted she could have heard me, even in the perfect silence around us.

I was just about to give up when her hand opened, slowly. The knife fell to the ground.

For the space of a second, our hands found each other with no barrier left.

The deer exhaled loudly from his nose. I snatched my hand back and took a few hesitant steps forward.

The deer was definitely on edge. I bowed my head lower, careful not to meet his eyes.

"It's ok," I crooned, keeping my hands up as I approached him, step by slow step.

"That's it, good boy." My technique seemed to be working: he no longer looked threatened, rather curious, his head tipped slightly to the side.

I was soon so close that I could've touched his horns, if only I extended my hand.

"Go, now, slowly, we need to keep him calm." I said to the figures behind me.

I heard Loelia's footsteps disappear as she retreated further into the meadow, but Artemis was still there. Her solid presence behind me was watching my every move.

I took a few steps back.

The distant sound of a fawn in need of help reached our ears.

The deer turned and followed it.

A few moments and he was gone, running after the cry for help.

I turned and stared at Artemis, her eyes no longer playful or entertained. She looked livid.

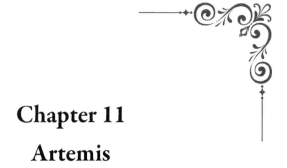

Chapter 11
Artemis

"THAT WAS EXTREMELY dangerous." My jaw was clenched and my heart hammered furiously against my chest "Animals are unpredictable."

"Not as unpredictable as you." She said, matching my angry expression "and what do you care anyway? I'm surprised you care so much about my safety, given the shitty way you've treated me since we first met."

"What do you mean?"

"Oh, you don't remember? 'I bite', 'I'm just going to sleep', random disappearances, random angry looks, 'here, look at how generous I am for giving you victory', barking orders. I have a whole list of them."

I felt myself grow hot at the injustice of it. "I don't care to appease to your lofty sense of good manners."

"Lofty? I don't think basic decency is really that hard to achieve."

"Perhaps we just have different standards." I retorted, trying to turn away. In her agitation she had come so close, I could have easily extended my arm and wrapped it around her waist. Not that I wanted to.

"You know what I think the problem is?" Human Callisto asked, her tone insisting that I wouldn't escape her any longer. "The problem is that your friend Eusachia enables your shitty behaviour instead of calling you out on it. No one dares call you out. But this is about to change."

"Oh yeah?"

"Yes, I'm so sick of it." She was holding her breath and looking at me intently. The heat of our conversation had charged the air between us. Her lips looked as soft as ever.

"C'mon give me your best, then."

Her tongue darted over her lips.

"...You're acting like an asshole."

"That's your best?"

She was quiet.

My eyes were still stuck on her lips.

And then, just like that, she turned around and started walking towards the meadow.

"Hey, I'm not done!" I shouted after her. I trailed behind the screaming "*I love you bear-y much, too*' printed on the back of her pyjama. The sparkly letters were catching slivers of moon light with every step.

"Too bad, because I am." she said, while her steps slowed down almost imperceptibly "You aren't the only one who gets to decide when to leave an uncomfortable situation"

"I am not going to apologise about the archery competition." I said, firmly.

"You" she turned, wielding her fingers at me like a sharp blade, "are incorrigible."

I took advantage of her temporary attention "Why did you do it?"

"What do you mean?"

"Why did you help her? Loelia. You never even talked to her, and yet you were willing to take such a huge risk for her. "

The surprise at my words won over her irritated frown. "Why wouldn't I do it?"

"What has she done to deserve it?"

"Just because you use sparingly the good manners you have, doesn't mean we all act this way" and with that Callisto was off, rushing off towards the meadow, sparing no more glances my way.

Talk to me. I wanted to say, but there was only so much dignity left in me, and I held on jealously to its remains.

We arrived at the meadow and were greeted by a lot of 'wows' and 'oh thank Zeus'.

Before either of us had time to take them in, the bolting figure of Loelia landed in front of me. She threw her arms around my neck "thank you for saving me, you're a hero." Her auburn hair tickled my nose.

"Loelia, what game are you playing?" I said tersely.

"Of course, thanks to you too, Hanna," she said, sparing a glance for the other woman.

"No need."

Callisto shoulders were still squared and tense.

"Not now," I said, with the intent of getting rid of the nymph.

I followed Callisto's eyes as they took in Loelia's semi-naked body under her sheer nightgown. After a moment, her gaze clouded and she deflated somewhat. "I agree," she said "it's late. You two lovebirds feel free to celebrate without me, I'm going back to the tent."

I tried to push Loelia off "We're not..-"

But the nymph put her hand over my mouth. "It will be easier this way," she whispered. Before I could bite her hand off and explain, Callisto had left, her steps drawing back further and further towards the tents.

"Get off me," I warned Loelia.

She complied.

I left Loelia in the meadow with the rest of the nymphs and headed towards the tent where human Callisto had disappeared just a minute earlier.

I did not wait for her invitation to speak. I wasn't sure I'd be given one either way. "I released the knife... despite my best instinct. Doesn't it count for something?"

The memory of her hand on mine sent a shiver through my body. How was it possible that I still desired her so much?

"Yeah, I saw that." Callisto seemed to hesitate a second before entering in her sleeping bag. "Carrying that knife, you were the one who put us all in danger. What do you expect, a thank you card?"

"What's that?"

"You are unbelievable. Goodnight." Callisto turned and close her eyes.

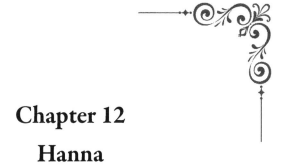

Chapter 12
Hanna

"HEY THERE." LOELIA took the seat in front of me in one fluid motion."That looks gorgeous," she said, pointing at the rainbow coloured bracelet mess I'd started.

"Not as creative as yours," I replied. Around her wrist, woven on a white base, stood the most detailed crafted hunting scene. Even a tiny bow and arrow had made its way through the thin bracelet. "Impressive work."

She smiled, waving her hand as to brush away the compliment. "I...just wanted to thank you properly for what you did last night."

"It was nothing special. "

"You saved my life."

I looked down on the floor, embarrassed, "the deer was just scared. I didn't do much, really."

Since last night there had been no traces of the angry little cloud Artemis anywhere. Which was fine by me. 100% ok.

"I have been thinking how to repay you, and I thought sharing a secret might be the way to go.."

"I am not really... wait. You said what?"

She smirked. "We have sauna facility at the campsite for the guest use, perhaps that could interest you and your friend?"

"Lori is asleep." I said, barely holding back the excitement."You said sauna?!".

"Yes, wanna go?" She pointed towards the woods.

"I'll go grab my swimsuit, then" I said, before she had a chance to change her mind.

Loelia smiled. "I'll wait for you here, then."

The campsite facilities apparently extended well beyond the main tent. On the side, behind the first rows of trees there was a previously hidden little cottage that hosted one of the most impressive hydromassage I had ever seen. Greek statues were dotted all around the edges of the warm pool, and in in the middle of it, a tall waterfall fell from the roof, crashing into the water underneath in a whirl of foam. The dim lights around, akin to torches, were casting dancing shadows on the wall, silent witness to the thundering water.

"Wow... that's.."

"Impressive isn't it?" Loelia's voice echoed in the elegant hall.

I turned to look at Loelia, only to find her disrobing. One fluid motion and her dress - a cotton white thing that poorly concealed her generous curves- was pooled at her feet. She was stark naked and every bit as curvaceous as I dreamt of being.

"Your turn."

I sent a silent insult to the human who had invented crisps and took off my shirt. My trousers fell on the floor soon after. Under Loelia watchful gaze, the tiny watermelon printed on my bathing suit appeared to be the most ridiculous choice I had ever made clothing-wise - at least, since I'd decided the shirt that said *straight until wet* was a worthwhile purchase. I felt my face heating up.

"Time for a sauna."

I was so relieved that I could hide in a dark and foggy cabin that I followed her without question. I entered the steamy room only for the rush of hot air to blind me on the spot.

"Oh, Artemis, what a coincidence. I was just thinking about you."

The woman, disrupter of my nightly dreams and regular intruder into my day ones, was lounging on one of the benches. She was wearing a white towel around her body, her complexion glistening with sweat. Her hair was messy and wet and I could imagine her hand playing with them, arranging them oh-so-casually in this 'I-just-fucked-someone' hairstyle.

She gave us a curt nod.

"Hope we can join you?" Loelia said, moving towards the woman with swaying hips. Even I was raptured by the elegant feline movement the woman could pull off. Artemis however seemed completely oblivious. To my surprise, the only glance she threw was in my direction, and for a second, just a second, I read a different sort of heat than usual in her eyes.

Loelia stroked her arm. Brave woman, indeed. The day I felt comfortable just caressing a woman this gorgeous would be the day I felt confident in my watermelon bikini, probably.

I sat near the steam stove, careful to avoid another blinding jet of hot air.

"So what have you been up to?" Loelia asked.

"Not much," she replied shortly. It was the first time I had heard a normal conversation taking place near her. The other women all seemed to treat her with the same jokey reverence you reserved for a mad king.

"I've missed you around."

The woman did not reply. She just sent another glance in my direction. Embarrassed, maybe? This woman was a full time job just to figure out.

"Have you ever heard of something called a tantric massage?" Loelia's hands had somehow reached her back, delicately kneading the muscles there.

"Loelia, please-"

The naked woman's hands fell to her sides, as her lips pursed in a pout "You're mean-"

"Nice day, huh?" I said, unable to stand there silently and awkwardly any longer.

"Mmm"

The tension was growing again. And my level of embarrassment with it.

"Have you been hiking around? Any good suggestions on where my friend and I could go?"

My eyes had fallen on Artemis shoulders' muscles. She was sitting sideways, so I had a wonderful, undisturbed view of her bulging bicep, inked with some tribal-looking patterns. Once more I was forced to acknowledge the sheer attractiveness of the woman. Her posture, even sitting, was regal.

"You are not skilled enough for those hikes" .

"I'll have you know I am actually a very skilled hiker" I replied indignant. No biceps in the world were going to make me feel like a newbie at this. I'd been hiking since I could stand on my own two feet. Who did this woman think she was?

She turned towards me "Oh really?" She said, mockingly.

"I am a pretty good hiker myself," Loelia interjected.

With Artemis' eyes firmly set on me, I felt a new surge of competitiveness rising inside "Yes, and I can prove it" I said perhaps a bit too boldly. "Pick a time and place and I'll race you to the top of any hill."

The temperature in the sauna seemed to have raised by a few degrees, because every breath was burning as if a dragon was blowing fire down my throat.

"No," she said lounging back in her sideways position.

"Well, someone's really scared, huh?"

This time when she turned, her eyes seemed on fire. She was staring at me with the look of someone who was about to actually bite. Her dark iris seemed to be growing bigger and bigger in front of my face.

"I need air-"

I pushed the door open and was immediately hit with the cold air of the room.

Water. I needed to cool down my body.

The pool, with its quiet tide and cooler temperature was inviting me in, winking at my spinning head.

I took a few steps "Never mind, I'm good-"

Leave her. This is your chance to let her go. I heard someone whisper behind me.

And the world went black.

"CALLISTO."

"What happened?"

"Oh dear!"

"She's waking up."

The voices were overlapping in a cacophony of sound. Through the painful thumping in my head, I forced my eyes to open.

Artemis' face was there, barely an inch from my own. Her eyes looked pained with unmistakably worry, fear even. Her arms were wrapped around me, the loud thumping of her own heart beating against my skin.

"Are you alright?"

I coughed hard, trying to speak. My throat was burning, convulsing with the need to expel water and inhale oxygen. Was I alright? What had happened to me?

"Give her space," Eusachia's authoritative voice said, sending those strong arms away from my reach. If I could only have protested, I would have.

A few more coughs shook through my lungs and I attempted to sit up.

Artemis was still staring at me. "What the hell happened?"

"Too much heat," Loelia had swooped into view and answered for me, pawing at Artemis. "If it wasn't for you, she wouldn't be breathing."

"Did you, really?" Eusachia said, surprised.

Artemis did not move except to brush Loelia off.

"I'm fine" I said with a raspy voice.

Before I had time to express my appreciation, Artemis had gotten on her feet. She was already halfway to the door, by the time a new cough fit had settled.

"Don't worry, dear, we'll get you back on the tent, safe and sound" Eusachia said.

"Please don't tell Lori" I said, feeling every word burn through my throat.

"No worries, your secret is safe with me." She said with a wink.

But my mind was already elsewhere: Artemis had saved me. She had. And God knew I had no idea why.

Chapter 13
Artemis

BY THE TIME I REACHED the Chow Hall, the enormous tent was already filled with laughter. My eyes were drawn straight to Hanna who was chatting away with a bunch of nymphs near the end of the candle-lit banqueting area. She looked.. healthy. The ridiculous candelabra floating above her was swaying a little, making the light in her eyes dance. I searched her face but could not detect a trace of the afternoon's misadventure: there were no bruises, nor wounds and I could hear her strong heartbeat all the way from where I was standing. Despite the steady rhythm, though, I could still see her hands fidgeting in her lap.

I imagined untangling her fingers, warming them against my own.

"No need to be nervous."

"I'm not nervous, I'm scared." Callisto said, staring at me imploringly "Actually, I'm terrified."

"Are you more scared that He is my Father or the Almighty God?"

"Both" Callisto's hands were playing restlessly "I think it's a bad idea."

"I know it's unprecedented" I caressed her skin, willing for my touch to ease her fear "but if He agrees, we could be together for the rest of eternity."

"We already can, remember? I am an immortal being too."

"You are not unwoundable, though. Anyone who wants to hurt me could just kidnap you and torture you until the end of time."

She looked up, incredulous, "What a pleasant, calming thought, love."
A sly smile framed her lips as I realised what I'd done. Her hand flew to
my cheek "I know you'd find me before it got that far, anyway."

"Of course." My hand gripped hers in earnest, "and the wrath descend-
ing upon them would be known as as the single most violent revenge ever
known among humans or Gods, I promise you." The blood was roaring in
my ears at the thought of anyone harming her. I could not let it happen.
That's why I'd begged her to see Zeus in the first place.

Callisto stared back at me, her fingers finally still. "Let's go then."

Hanna's eyes met mine.

I couldn't look away, nor find peace when my eyes were focused
anywhere else. Was it the need to ensure her safety? Was it her eyes
helplessly glittering under the candle light? Or was I just mad? Truly
and utterly mad.

I finally pulled my eyes away from Hanna and took in the full scene
around me.

The table was laden with enough food for a feast on Mount Olympus: there was warm bread, varieties of cheese, olives, pheasant and par-
tridge, eggs from both quails and hens, legumes, vegetables, figs. The
smell was equally divine.Yet, I found I had lost my appetite.

Eusachia stood, her glass in one hand, a glinting knife in the other.

She brought the two together and eventually the noise gathered
everyone's attention.

"Welcome everyone, including those who have not joined us previously." She shot a look in my direction. "One of the Happy Campers,
Sarisi, has kindly offered to read us one of her enchanting poems ac-
companied with the Lyra, an Ancient Greek musical instrument that
many say has the power to hypnotise. So...be careful ladies."

With a wink, Eusachia passed the attention to Sarisi who, poised
on a small platform at the head of the table, began strumming the long
delicate strings of the Lyra. The sound of the music washed over me, the
notes untangling the knots in my chest one by one.

" *It's no use*
   Mother dear, I
   can't finish my
   weaving
   You may
   blame Aphrodite
   soft as she is
   she has almost
   killed me with
   love for that girl"

My eyes were burning as I fought the tears that threatened to spill out.

I remembered. It was the night I had whispered my pain to Sappho, quietly, in her ear, in the middle of the night. Dionysus had got me drunk on Ambrosia, and then let me scream and drink and cry until none of his courtiers were left to witness my unravelling. When I had finally exhausted myself I had fallen, at once silent, on the marble floor.

"Are you done?"

"You couldn't understand"

"Why do you think I've been rolling in women and alcohol all this time?" He'd said, calm as ever, never raising to my bait, and filling another cup of ambrosia.

"You couldn't know about this kind of hurt: you're the God of ecstasy and celebration."

"No-one, not even a God, has that much to celebrate."

Dionysus was a small creature with soft features. Under the right light, nobody would guess him more than a boy. He was indulgent- with himself mostly- and most considered his brain too weakened by alcohol consumption to ever produce sound advice.

I'd always known better.

"What should I do?" I'd asked him, my eyes were red but dry at this point. Somewhere amongst the pitying looks I'd received during the last few hours I'd resolved to never shed another tear over this nymph again. I couldn't stand it.

Instead of laughing, as he might have, Dionysus had opened his arms wide. "Joined me here, then. We'll have fun forever."

"I can't."

"Then go write music, or poetry, or start sewing like your sexually frustrated sister does."

"Athena is sewing now?"

He had rolled his eyes. "New fad. Very obsessed. She turned a woman into a spider."

"Sounds dreadful," All I could think of was Callisto's hand weaving my hair.

"Maybe you could try turning a human into a lizard?" He said, sipping from the cup. "Nah, never mind. I think they tried a while ago. Your dad called them Dinosaurs. It didn't work."

Tearing off a piece of the tablecloth, he passed the fabric to me and I blew my nose.

"... I'm not the sort of dramatic being who writes poetry about my ex."

"Honey, I don't know how to tell you but... from where I am standing, you are every bit that dramatic."

Another pitiful smile. It seemed like I'd spent two millennia collecting them.

The memory dissolved and I stood from the chair. The sound, squeaky and sudden halted Sarisi's hands. Her eyes darted towards me.

I did not wish to quiet her, nor indeed any nymph in the crowd. I simply wanted to vanish like I'd hoped to at the time of my conversation with Dionysus. I wanted to disappear so that nobody could look at me with pity.

Especially not Hanna.

As I rushed through the door, head down, hiding the tears that had finally won the battle. I felt her gaze, weighing more than the columns of Hercules on my shoulders.

"This was wonderful Sarisi, thank you for such a moving performance," I heard Eusachia say behind me.

I could not go in the forest, Nerea would surely find me there and I did not want to hear one more sermon from her or Eusachia about the mess I was making of this appalling camping trip.

I headed to the tent instead, thinking that I could pretend to be asleep by the time Hanna returned for the night.

I fell onto my sleeping back and sank into the relief of being alone, finally.

"Are you inside?" Hanna whispered.

I lay quietly, surprised by the early disturbance of my peace.

"If you need to talk... talking helps."

I wasn't entirely sure human Callisto was gay until this moment.

"Can I come in or will you bite me?" Hanna asked, the caution in her voice making it clear that she was only half-joking.

"Yes, you can come in."

She bent forward and clumsily crossed the threshold. A mountain of food was only barely balanced on the plate in her hands "I brought you small selection" she smiled, handing it over.

"Why?"

"I saw you eyeing it before, but was sure you hadn't had a bite, you seemed so taken by the music." She extended her arms, driving her plate closer to me. "Those ladies are animals when they eat, especially the yoga teacher. I was worried that there would be nothing left by the time you snuck in later to get it."

"No. I mean, why?"

The plate, a precarious peace offering, stood between us.

"You saved my life. I got you a plate of food. I think that evens us out." That wry smile of hers peeked out again.

I grabbed the plate. "I'm not sure that's how it works."

"Excuse me, food is necessary for survival and so is avoiding drowning in a pool. Logically, it makes perfect sense."

I took a bite of the pheasant. "Thank you"

She smiled, a proper one this time.

"So, what's her name?"

"Mmm?"

"The woman who hurt you."

"No-one hurt me."

"Sure, ok, I'll tell you mine then. Her name was Finley."

I almost spit out the bite of pheasant in my mouth. *Finley?!? Who the hell was Finley?!*

The corner of her mouth twitched and a thin layer of sadness glazed her eyes, "I was in pain too, you know."

The thought of a human Finley, somewhere, at some point, kissing Hanna was... upsetting. More than that, infuriating. I heard thunder in the distance. Someone was definitely having an unprecedented wet summer.

"It still hurts a bit. Ok, a lot. But I worked through it."

I followed the curve of her neck, a cone of moonlight casting shadows on her face. Even in the dark, those eyes sparkled like the blade of an arrow. I am sure, had Artemis spell not prevented her from learning the truth, she would have read the feelings for Callisto as plain as day. My soft, beautiful, fierce Callisto.

"It takes time," she added.

It's been two thousand years, love, and you are still a blow to the stomach.

Someone ripped the zip at the entrance open. "Hey" Hanna's human friend, bursting in waving a headband "What's happening in here?"

A stir of anger blossomed within me. Not quite anger, something akin to bitterness. *Jealousy.* I heard Aphrodite whispering in my head.

To Hades with that.

"It's fine Lori, really." Hanna said, shooting a look at me, "She's all bark and no bite."

She offered a tentative smile.

Then got up and looked at her friend "Let's go finish dinner."

The night air would have usually cleared my head of uncomfortable thoughts, but this time, as the breeze came in behind her form leaving the tent I felt something worse. *Rejected*, Aphrodite suggested again, as I reached for the hunks of cheese and bread on the plate.

I felt rejected.

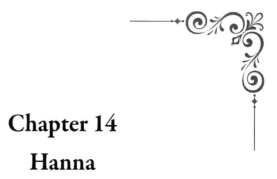

Chapter 14
Hanna

I WENT BACK INTO THE tent an hour later with a churning stomach.

I had talked too much.

I should have kept quiet.

What was I even thinking? Perhaps it was the cognac Eusachia had given me *for good measure* after the sauna incident.

All I wanted to do was... make Artemis feel less alone? I knew what a broken heart felt like. I knew that the worst part is often not the break up or the cheating itself. It's the way you bury your head in the sand as you ignore the break up unfolding over the months prior. You ignore how she stops making you coffee in the morning and stops touching you at night. How she talks enthusiastically about one person in particular and how they start going out together night after night -*babe, don't be jealous* - and you're not because why would you be? But you are.

You see her changing and try harder.

Fights and promises.

Until the day your world falls apart and you are left there, thinking, *of course*.

I tiptoed inside. Artemis was turned away from me and I couldn't see her eyes to know if she was awake or not. She wasn't a fan of company, though, I knew that much about her. I tucked in the uncomfortable sleeping bag, and changed into my ridiculous pyjamas. I could hear the peaceful sound of the wind tickling the trees nearby. An owl hooted. I adjusted my back against the thin mattress and closed my eyes.

"I think anger might be more productive" Artemis said, interrupting the silence.

I looked over to her, forgetting sleep entirely, "What do you mean?"

"What you said about working through it. I think anger might help with that."

"And where would it get you?" I asked.

"It's easier to be angry than sad."

"I don't have it in me, I think," I said after a moment in silence. "It's not a comfort for me to wish her bad."

Artemis seemed to think this through, the silence growing again until it filled the space between us. I felt a change in her posture and demeanour, "who's Finley?"

There seemed to be a hint of anger in her words, or possessiveness. I shook away the silly thought.

"My ex, of course," I said smiling in an attempt to lighten up the heaviness I felt hanging in the air, "isn't it always an ex?"

"Did she hurt you?" She asked.

"She did. I found her in our bed with her coworker, one day when I came back unexpectedly early from work."

I felt a wave of anger in Artemis as if it boiled in my own veins.

"What would you do to her if you could, then?" She asked as if there was truly something that could be done.

"There's no point in wishing upon a star".

"But if you could express a wish?"

"I'd wish that she wasn't still happy with that girl, I think. I'd be ok with her being happy with anyone else, but not her. I find it unfair."

"That's it?" Artemis asked. "That's all you'd wish for?" She propped on her elbow and looked at me. I could feel the gaze on my skin ever in the pitch black darkness. "You wouldn't want her to be eaten alive by alligators, or burned on the stake?"

"That sounds a bit intense, doesn't it?" I said with a laugh. Artemis sure had her own sense of humour. I found I liked it. "No, if I wished for that, it would mean I never truly loved her, don't you think?"

That really seemed to give Artemis pause, as if she'd never considered things from that perspective.

"I think Love is often one sided and problematic...but I do think it's real and...timeless" I added.

"So you still love this woman?" She broke out of her reverie suddenly.

"Maybe, maybe not. I think it's easier to idolise people in your memory after a long period of loneliness."

I'm not lonely I thought I heard the other woman murmur, but I couldn't be sure.

"So what's your sob story?" I asked. "An ex?"

"She slept with my dad."

"Holy Cow." I said in shock "I'm so sorry." I was petrified. Who would do such a messed up thing? "Perhaps roasting on a stake wouldn't be too much in your case," I said, only half joking."No wonder you're so angry."

"I mean it was a bit more complicated than that, but yes, that's what happened."

"Do you still talk to your Father?"

"I don't really have a choice about that."

I looked at her. Outside the crickets were singing and I was eager to be a bit closer. "You always have a choice," I said.

There was silence from her other side, and I knew it was time to be quiet. Artemis had turned around again and given me her shoulder. Perhaps she was more like me than I gave her credit for.

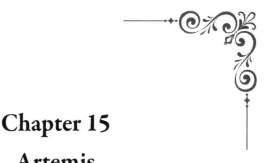

Chapter 15

Artemis

I opened my eyes.

I had slept.

I didn't even need sleep: I was a Goddess, for Olympus' sake.

Hanna was resting peacefully next to me. The sound of her soft snoring eased my furious heartbeat. Luckily, nobody had found us here, defenceless.

Nothing bad had happened. She was alright. Truly.

I took a deep breath and closed my eyes.

Those damn crickets chirping away in the dark must have lulled me into losing consciousness.

I got up and the memories of the previous night lunged at me at once. *If I wished for that, it would mean I never truly loved her, don't you think?*

I looked at Hanna's sleeping figure. Had she really known love in her short human life?

A pang of anger stabbed at my stomach, as my eyes desperately searched for the truth in her curled up position, the rising and falling of her chest, her soft lips.

It was always easier for them, I guess. Humans. All they had - if they were lucky - was seventy or so years and a faulty memory. It made it easier to move on and live with no regrets. As a Goddess, I could not enjoy the same privileges: my memory was ironclad, and my loneliness was a given.

I tiptoed outside. The cold air of the night lashed at my face and a shiver went running through my body.

It must be said that humans had changed in the past few millennials.

Before, they used to fear us and beg for our benevolence. We used to matter: the destiny of so many was held in our hands. But ever since the Almighty God's grip had diminished, we had lost our purpose.

What was the point of looking down? What was the point of righting wrong? The interventions were ignored anyway. Sending miracles? The mortals interpreted them as just blind luck. Curses? They were shrugged off as superstitions. *Tomorrow will be better.*

Either way we were irrelevant. Nothing but myths and tales of capricious beings.

Callisto would know what to say in this moment. She'd take my hand and look into my eyes "Don't do it for them. Do it for you."

And I would have believed I still mattered, at least while the sparkle in her eyes held my heart hostage.

I sighed. It was unhealthy to be around humans for so long. That was for sure.

The bow and arrow Nerea had given me was hidden under a blanket of leaves at the edge of the meadow. I uncovered it and crossed the nearby river, jumping on the slippery rocks that castellated the powerful flow of water. Despite the darkness, my eyes were as careful as ever, so I found it easy to spot my target: it was dangling in the night breeze, ripe and ready to be caught. I aimed.

The wind was perpendicular to the trajectory of my arrow so I aimed right. Shot.

I heard, from miles away, the sound of the luscious bunch of berries falling to the ground and, in a quick dash, I reached the bleeding fruit. My arrow was stabbing a few tantalising pearls of sweetness.

I saw it and understood.

It was time to move on, and stop shooting random berries in the middle of the night.

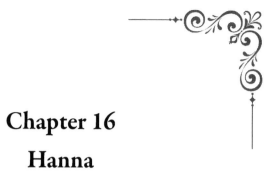

Chapter 16
Hanna

RENEWED ENERGY WASHED over me when I finally opened my eyes. Predictably, Artemis was not in the tent. For once, though, her absence did not make me suspicious she was planning my murder somewhere. I called that progress.

The sky was as clear as ever, despite the awful weather predictions the day before.

I gathered my things quickly and headed straight for the main tent where a breakfast table was laden with far more than just the usual sorts of food.

"What's going on?"

"It's the one week celebration," Sarisi said, dashing past me with an oversized plate.

"Do we celebrate that?" I asked.

"I mean, you survived a near drowning" Lori had appeared in front of me with a stoney expression on her face. "So a week in this place might be worth a celebration"

"Lori, I am sorry I didn't tell you, I was worried you'd-"

"No, no, there's no problem, I know why you didn't say anything" She grabbed my arm and pushed me into one of the tent nooks. "But at least now you believe me" She whispered.

"Believe what?"

"That this a cult and if we don't convert to their religion, they'll kill us."

"Right, and what kind of religion would that be?"

"Have you heard the sheer amount of *Oh Zeus* they exhale at every moment? This is some kind of ancient greek religion. I'm calling it."

"Lori."

"Hanna."

I stared back at her, "Then why did Artemis rescue me? I never converted to any religion."

"She did what?"

"She rescued me. Ms Broody Butch. She was the one that got me out of the pool."

"Maybe she's rebelling against the Order...we'd be foolish to trust her quite so soon, though. Keep your eyes on her."

"Lori this is not Hunger Games."

"I know *that*," she said, rolling her eyes. "This is not fiction. This is life or death."

I took a deep breath. "Lori-"

"Attention everyone!" Eusachia voice burst from the front of the tent. "To celebrate the end of the first week at the Happy Camper All Women's retreat I have organised an epic treasure hunt for all of you to enjoy."

Artemis entered the tent at that moment, looking as handsome as ever. Her eyes travelled to mine. They were not angry, nor disdainful, as I had come to expect of her on these occasions. They were.. timid? Skittish? They kept dancing between me and the floor, vulnerability painted all over. My breath caught somewhere in my chest.

Did she regret our talk? I wanted to approach her, to ask her if everything was alright.

I could be a friend to her, I thought, if that's what she needed. All I had to do would be try to ignore her bulging biceps and sculpted fea tures. And forget the way my stomach dived down below it's allocated place, at a thousand miles an hour, whenever she was around me.

I could do it.

I could.

"..Each tent will be given a map. Follow the path marked on it and try to arrive first to the final location. If you do.. there will be a prize waiting for you"

Tentmates, then. Would Artemis want to participate?

"What's the final prize, you ask?" Eusachia teased the perfectly quiet audience. "Other than the great company, of course," She raised her coffee mug higher "..a handy toy to be used for single or double pleasure"

What?!?

The rest of the women remained silent, but the energy in the tent had definitely changed.

"Is this a gay retreat?" Lori whisper-yelled in my ear.

I looked at Eusachia. Her smile was still plastered on her face, betraying no sign of her words being a joke. Then, of their own accord, my eyes travelled to Artemis, who's petrified expression told me everything I needed to know about her enthusiasm about winning the prize.

Not that I was thinking about it. Because I wasn't.

One of the ladies coughed, breaking the silent spell.

"Very good then," Eusachia smiled and sat back down.

"Have you considered this might make some of the guests uncomfortable?" It was Artemis, brave in a sea of silence, who dared to speak.

Which also meant my theory was right. Sex was the furthest thing from Artemis' mind. Uncomfortable, was the word she had used. Which was great. Perfect, even. Because I wanted to be strictly friendly.

"Thank you for raising your concern." Eusachia replied in a way that made it very clear she was not thankful in the slightest " It is however all in good fun and spirit and it's not meant to suggest anything in particular"

"Thank Goddess" Artemis spoke again "Imagine if you were attempting to be suggestive."

I chuckled. So did many of the other women. Including Lori.

"Thank you for the lovely laugh, Artemis," Eusachia said with a pointed look in her direction. "And now that all concerns have been raised, please head to your tent where you'll find instructions on the day's activity"

"LOOK, WE DON'T HAVE to do this at all. Especially if you are uncomfortable. It is just a suggested activity, not a law. I can go for a dried flower composition class, you can run away in the woods. And it will be absolutely, completely fine. Peachy fine."

The rush of heat was growing in my face. I took a deep breath. I had recited the whole stream of words in one go, leaving no space for air. *Be cool.* I told myself.

Artemis was staring at me with a questioning look. Pondering, probably, whether I was crazy.

"I asked it for you. Back then, I mean," she said at last.

"Oh.. Oh. You mean, you didn't want me to be embarrassed."

She shrugged, "if you are."

"I am not. I am cool. It's not like it's a suggestion to do something.."

Her eyes darted to the floor "No, of course.." She studied my expression again "..so are you alright?"

"No.. yes. Of course, I am alright. One hundred percent."

"Good" she opened the map Eusachia had left on our pillow. The instructions were almost offensively simple: a trick. All we had to do was follow the river until we'd cross the path. Less than a mile up and then back. Kid's play.

I prepared our bag in silence. I packed my first aid kit and rolled in a blanket for good measure.

"So you ready?" Artemis asked, peaking from behind my shoulder. The way she accidentally grazed my arm tied my stomach in a knot. I craved that familiarity.

"Yep"

"Good" She replied, crossing the threshold of our tent.

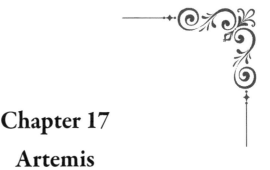

Chapter 17
Artemis

"I THOUGHT YOU DIDN'T like group activities." Hanna said with a sideways glance. I could hardly hear her over the babbling river and my laboured steps as we moved further into the woods and up another hill.

We had yet to meet another participant.

"Two people hardly constitute a group," I replied, trying hard not to stare at Hanna, at least while she seemed interested in looking at me.

She was wearing very short shorts.

It was distracting.

"This way" I said, as I caught sight of the path ahead. I'd been here many times in the first few days of camping, always in solitude, and I'd learned that the place was made so that you could never be further than a certain distance from the centre. It was a maze that would lead you back to familiar ground.

"I can't see it."

"Just a bit further ahead, there."

Her eyes squinted, searching for the pebbled road I was pointing at.

"You have good eyesight. I can't see anything," she replied.

I shrugged.

"So, what do you like to do in your spare time?" She asked, changing the subject.

"I used to ride a lot. Hunting." Men mostly. They were my specialty. I thought it inappropriate to mention, though.

If the vegetarian in her felt repulsed at my hobby, she did not show it.

"Why do you say 'used to'?" She asked instead.

"Humans flooded the place and suddenly there was not a single piece of land where I could ride in peace with my... friends."

She halted on the path "Humans?"

"It's the name of my Father's development." I said "Humans, inc."

"Curious name. I've never heard of it."

"It's quite well known back in Greece."

"Oh.. that makes sense. You have a different...aura to you. It must be the mediterrean sun."

"It's miraculous, indeed," I said deadpan.

"So, wait a second," she halted again. I could see that, despite her efforts to conceal it, she was a bit sweaty. "Your Father, not only did he do what he did with your ex," she swallowed as she caught sight of my expression, "but he also destroyed the place you felt most comfortable in? Wow. Someone should give him the Father of the year award."

Not my favourite topic, for sure.

"Sorry" she said, noticing my discomfort.

Was I really that easy to read?

"What about your Father?" I asked.

Her apologetic expression was swiftly replaced by one of sadness. "My dad died from cancer a year ago, right before I caught Finley in the affair."

"I am so sorry."

She offered me a sad smile.

"I was lucky, though. My dad was wonderful. He taught me how to enjoy the outdoors and make great barbecues. Of course, then I turned vegetarian. So that didn't stick."

"He sounds pretty great" I said.

The smile she gave me this time was bigger. It reached her eyes.

She wiped the sweat off her face with the sleeve of her shirt. I had a quick vision of her sweaty skin on mine, as we used to indulge ourselves after a great hunt.

She turned her gaze ahead, "I see it. The path. We're almost there!"

She grabbed my wrist for a moment. Her warm touch, however brief, sent shivers through my skin, an electric shock both familiar and exciting. I felt at once light and heady, like after a good glass of ambrosia.

I barely noticed the road for the final mile we walked together.

And then at once we both stopped as we'd been given the same silent cue. I stood there, feeling caught, in front of the most ridiculous display of a sex toy ever known to mankind.

"*Need a hand?*" Said the wooden plank drilled into the tree.

From one of its branches, dangling below, hung the purple penis-shaped object.

To complete the picture, "*Hope you enjoyed the ride*" was drawn on the ground beneath the tree.

It looked disturbingly similar to a three years old art project, featuring an adult sex toy, made by someone with a questionable sense of humour. It was either Eusachia's idea or my sister's: they were as bad as each other, really.

I rolled my eyes.

"Should I..?" Hanna asked, uncertain.

"Sure, be my guest."

She quickly undid the knot holding the dildo in place and stuffed the object down into her bag.

It was, I hoped, the last we'd see of it. Hanna's eyes seemed to say the same as they were hiding from mine, firmly planted on the ground.

"Wanna go for a swim?" I asked. It was a sudden idea, but one I thought was likely to get us both over the burning embarrassment of my sister meddling.

"The river?" She asked, eyeing the road we came from. "Isn't it too shallow?"

At last she was back to looking at me. I liked it better that way.

"Good enough for a bath, though."

She smiled wryly. "Race you to it." Before I could even decipher her words, she'd started running down the path. In what, I was sure, was an impressive performance for a human.

Too bad I wasn't going to play fair.

I couldn't help but smirk as she reached the river panting, far behind myself. "How?!?"

"Took a shortcut."

"That's cheating."

"No, it's not. You just said we had to get here, not which way to go."

She stood there, hands on her waist, looking at me angrily through the heaving breaths "Fine. I will concede you victory." she said in a very poor imitation of my voice.

"Good, very gracious of you" I bowed.

Hanna gave me the side-eye, but I could see the shadow of a smile in it.

I started peeling off my clothes. The shirt- what a ridiculous piece of clothing- went first and then my pants, until I was stark naked.

"Ohhh," When I turned, Hanna was staring at me, agape. To my disappointment, her garments were still on. The water was lapping at the hem of her pants, "You meant a naked bath."

"Do you usually take baths with your clothes on?"

I saw her swallow, "Are people in Greece that comfortable with nudity?"

I'd forgotten that humans were squeamish about it.

To be perfectly honest, the last time a human had seen me naked, I had had to turn him into a deer and hunt him down for fourteen days. All for a "breech of consent"- as Athena had called it during her weekly feminist theories lectures.

Anyway, Callisto had her eyes firmly on the water and seemed awfully embarrassed, playing restlessly with the hem of her shirt.

"If you want I can put my clothes back on," I said, feeling like an idiot.

"No, no it's ok." She said, her hands resting at last " I mean...I don't mean to say I want to see you naked or anything-"

"I didn't assume such a thing"

"Ok" She took a deep breath.

"You sure you are okay?"

"Yes, I think I am just going to stay here, on the bank of the river, if that's ok. You enjoy yourself."

"I have a better proposition," I said, feeling more daring all at once, "What about you close your eyes. I get into the water, so then you don't have to worry about me catching you staring at me."

Her eyes grew two sizes "Oh, you think I'm worried I am not going to be able to resist the urge to look at you naked?" There was a competitive edge to her words.

Here we go.

"Precisely." I turned. "Time to close your eyes." I walked into the water and laid down in its gentle current.

"You know what?" Hanna said. I raised my head and saw her taking off her shirt "Naked is totally fine" and with that battle cry, she threw away the rest of her clothes, one by one, until she was fully naked in front of me.

I would consider myself a gentlewoman in most circumstances, really. But I had a hard time taking my eyes off of her. Her nipples, hard from the gush of wind hitting her body were darker and erect, waiting to be sucked on. I allowed my eyes to travel further south were the curve of her belly softly faded into the space between her legs. I wished for nothing more than lick at every inch of her skin and feel her mold into my arms, once more.

Do you not remember me, Callisto? I thought.

She must have noticed my stare, because her shoulders curved as if to protect themselves from my eyes and then she sat right in the water, until only her neck and head broke past the surface of the water.

It made little difference though: the water was so clear that we could both see easily see every detail of our naked bodies even from where we stood.

"You train a lot, huh?"

"Excuse me?" I had to concentrate hard to get my eyes to move up to her face, finally.

"You got to the gym a lot...like sports?"

"Yeah, quite a bit I guess."

Looking at her, I found her in a guarded yet equally eager examination of my own skin."I can tell" she said before her eyes fell once more to an indeterminate spot in the water.

I bit my lips, "I run a lot, hikes, that sort of thing."

She nodded, while keeping her gaze still far away from my body. The little temptress in my brain, which disturbingly sounded a lot like my sister, was eager for Hanna to look at me again, to indulge in the sight of me at her leisure.

Did she not know that very few humans were still alive after seeing me naked? Because she should.

"How do you find the water?" I asked

"Delicious-" she said before putting her hand to her mouth in horror "I meant pleasant."

I smiled sly "I'm glad to hear that."

Chapter 18

Hanna

WHAT IN GOD'S NAME has happened to me?

Delicious.

My face was burning with shame.

Ok, perhaps I had been staring a bit too long at the woman. She was sculpted, like an actual greek statue, her body was the perfect blend of soft and hard. I imagined her pulling me against her, while her fingers worked inside me strong and deep.

No wonder that dumb thing came out of my mouth. Honestly, I would almost feel embarrassed about my own body if it wasn't that I had caught her staring at me several times without any attempt to hide it, really.

A player gotta play, I guess.

Still, it was flattering.

"When did you know?" I asked, eager to break the growing silence.

"Know what?"

"That you liked women?"

She seemed taken aback by the question. Good, two could play at that game. "I guess it's always gone unsaid. I have two sisters, and while one was running after every man she could find, the other was doing the same but with books. I liked neither, and just did my own thing."

"Is that code for playing the lesbian field?"

"According to the family's legend I'm still a virgin, so who's to know? Certainly a gentlewoman wouldn't say." She said with a smirk.

I knew she was a player. She was too handsome not to be, and I felt silly for even thinking that a woman like her could entertain the thought of..well, me.

Artemis seemed to notice my embarrassment at the revelation. "There was only one woman I loved though," she said, looking at me. She was staring deep into my eyes, as if searching for that memory from the depth of my own brain.

"Was it..?"

"Yes. Her name was Callisto and you are right, I had forgiven her a long time ago, because I did truly love her."

There was a moment of silent as a meditative moment quietly passed between us. I didn't understand what she meant fully nor was I expected to. But I knew in that moment something precious had gone through us, and for a second, I thought I'd seen the real Artemis, not the player, grumpy version of her.

And then that moment was gone.

"How about you?" She said, breaking the silence.

"I found out later. Uni, as cliches go. It all made sense at once."

She smiled. "Lots of fun, I imagine"

"Not as much fun as one with *friends* to ride away with might guess."

"We all had a wild youth, didn't we?"

I chuckled. The electricity between Artemis and I was crackling loudly. I lay in the water, floating through the current. There were no clouds and my hand shot up to screen my eyes from the blinding sun.

I felt alive in the water with her. I had the feeling of being.. familiar. Exciting and comfortable. Wild and safe. I no longer saw her as the hard shelled untouchable woman I had met, but more like the tender cored human I longed to get to know better.

In the end it was Artemis who left the river first, the ripples of water falling of her skin like beads of pearl.

"It's time for us to get moving," she said.

She got back to her clothes and put them on again, gingerly, grimacing at the feeling of her wet skin under the cotton. The sound of a cuckoo came from the forest. She stopped mid way through pushing her shirt over here head. I was going to miss the view.

"Something's off," she said.

"It was just a cuckoo."

"No, no, something else." Lines of worry were drawn over her face.

"I can't believe you of all people would be spooked by a bit of noise from the forest." I said teasingly. For a second I thought she was going to retort something spiteful, the way she used to do. But then her expression softened, "You're right, I'm worrying for nothing."

I got out of the water and put my clothes back on. In the process I felt self-conscious, a nugget of doubt biting at the edge of my comfort with the other woman.

It was just a cuckoo, I reminded myself.

We headed back to the main road and kept striding forward.

SEVEN HOURS LATER, we were still following the path. I could have sworn we'd been through the same spot at least a dozen times, but somehow, despite following the road, we'd keep moving further away from camp. We'd tried deviating from it, and the forest had gotten more and more dense until it was impossible to keep going.

Even the weather had turned. Heavy cloud threatened a heavy shower.

To make matters worse, my stomach had been rumbling for close to four hours. Artemis on the other hand, seemed untouched by both the effort and hunger. We had a light packed lunch with us but that had been finished four hours ago and the extent of the physical exercise had taken its toll.

"Blueberries" I said excitedly when we found a bush at the side of the road.

With both hands I picked the berries and shoved them into my mouth. They were juicy and delicious, quite different from the supermarket version you could find in the city.

"Here" I said handing a few over to her.

She looked at them suspiciously and then nabbed at one with a scrunched up face. "I'll admit, they are nice," She said and attempted a half smile in my direction.

"You know my father used to bribe me with this when I was young. Every berry was five minutes of walking."

"That seems quite a poor deal," she said, laughing.

"It was, that's why I occasionally stole a few from the back of his bag pocket," I said with a wink. I felt as giddy as back then. The berries had been like an emotional lift in the midst of the tiredness.

FINALLY, I GAVE IN.

"I'm setting up the tent."

It was close to midnight and we had walked for hours. While Artemis looked like she could keep going, I could not: my legs were aching and my back was screaming.

The tent had been quite a curious discovery as well, since I didn't remember putting it in my bag, yet there it was.

Artemis did not argue.

We got to work together and soon it was up and ready.

"That looks great!" I said "I mean, we are lost, sure, but at least we're not going to sleep rough."

"Mmm," Artemis was distracted. She had been since I'd suggested the tent. It seemed odd. I mean, we had bathed naked, how was sharing a slightly smaller tent than our usual one any more uncomfortable for her?

"Are you happy with the tent set up?" I asked.

"Yes, yes of course." The lines on her face had not disappeared, if anything they had deepened, over the course of the last few hours. "I am just confused about our direction." She opened the map once more and traced back with her finger on the road.

I knew without looking again that it was inexplicable. "They'll find us tomorrow morning," I said trying to soothe her. "I'm sure we're probably just around the corner and we got distracted along the way."

"You don't seem worried at all."

"What's the alternative, Miss Broody?" I said jokingly. I realised, once more too late, what I had said.

"Miss Broody?"

"Your old look, you know? Like *here I am, the queen of darkness, coming to eat your heart.*"

She smiled. It hadn't happened in a while. "I'm not like this with you," she said, sounding regretful about it anyway.

"No, you're not," I agreed, " not anymore, at least."

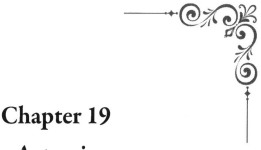

Chapter 19
Artemis

"THE HONOUR IS YOURS," Hanna said, gesturing towards the tent.

The tension between the two of us was palpable and real, and my heart ached for the desire to hold her tight.

However, I knew I couldn't. Shouldn't, really.

Not to mention, I was also pissed off with my sister. There was no way I would get the directions wrong. I was the Goddess of Woods, the forests are my own and following a path is something a three year old human child could do without failure.

I knew this was my sister trying to set us up. Even the sex toy was offensive. How could she believe I wasn't capable of taking care of the carnal pleasure of a woman without human objects? Not that I was planning to. Obviously.

Once inside the temperature seemed to drop. The puff of Callisto's breath hung in the air as she tried to warm herself up through energetic pats on her forearms.

"How are you not cold right now?" She asked. "You're from Greece."

"I lived up on the mountains there and we were used to low temperatures."

97

It was hard not to cover the distance between the two of us, and gather Callisto close to me. I felt pain seeing her shiver. Humans were so delicate. Back on the Olympus, Callisto and I used to race each other to the top, near the glaciers, nothing but a layer of flimsy cotton covering our bodies. Up and down we would run until I'd catch her and we would tumble over the side of the mountain, covered in dirt and laughing until someone came to find us.

Human Callisto -Hanna- instead had no such physical strength, she was subject to diseases and wounds, infections and hunger. I thought of how hard it would be to turn my eyes away from her, once I was back on the Olympus and trying to ignore the obstacles she would face in that delicate shell of a body.

"Do you miss Greece?"

I was not expecting this question. It took me a long time to think it over. "I miss how easy life is there for me. Very few things can touch me up there."

She looked at me expectantly.

"When I'm there it feels like nothing ever changes. There's nothing to experience, but, when I come back down here, it is all... difficult. There's pain and hurt. Everything you hear, everything you experience is moulded by human suffering."

"I think I know what you mean," she said, to my surprise, "back home, before my father passed at least, things never changed. It was all perfectly still. Safe. Like a bubble rather than reality. And then when I'm back in the city, it's all noises, and bad news, and the harsh realities of my job."

"You're a vet, right?"

"Yes. I'm often given the most gruesome cases, pets who are at the end of the line, really. I thought the job would be different: rescuing animals, nursing them back to health. But unfortunately death is more frequent than I'd like to admit."

Death was not something I'd usually indulge thinking on. It was a fate for humans, designed to make sure they'd never grown more powerful than us.

"I think death might be a gift at times," I said. The words surprised me. I had never intended to share such a thought with anyone, let alone a human. "When you live forever and there's no stakes and no fear, everything tastes only half as good. But when everyday could be your last, you're forced to take life into your own hands and make something that matters out of it."

I saw Callisto's eyes glistening in the dark. She was looking at me intrigued and a bit in awe, as if the thought had never occurred to her, yet my words made perfect sense.

"So you think it is that same fear of death that makes life meaningful?"

"Precisely."

How was it still so easy to talk to her?

She seemed to think it over for a second. Her shivering had subsided, I noticed. Yet her lips looked a pale mauve. I wanted to kiss them.

"I disagree," she said, "fear of death is so great that it's paralysing for many people."

"Not for you?" I asked. There was a warmth at the edge of my stomach that was spreading through my limbs. It was a familiar feeling, yet it felt brand new.

"Sometimes," she said, surprising me once more. "But there's really no alternative than coming to terms with it."

I fell quiet.

"What do you do?" She asked, "to rid yourself of the fear of dying?"

I realised too late that perhaps my opinion meant nothing. What could I know? I would never know death.

"I'm never going to die," I said, honestly.

It made her laugh. The sound reverberated through the tent. It scared an owl that fluttered away from a nearby branch. "Denial. I see, smart," she said, at last.

"That's what I do best" I said, smiling. I was glad she didn't take my line too seriously.

I heard the growl from her belly. She must have been starving by now. "Sorry" she said, clenching her stomach.

I felt an urge to protect her. A human. No, my human. Even though perhaps that would have come across as presumptuous and possessive in equal measure. "Do you want me to get you something?"

"How?"

"I am a great huntress."

"Vegetarian, remember?" She said scrunching up her face. "How are you not hungry?" She held her finger up in the air "No, wait, I know this one. There was no food when you grew up in Greece, so you learned how to make do?"

A chuckle escaped my lips, before I could stop it. I pursed my lips. "There was food in Greece," I clarified.

I did not see her smile, but I could guess it.

"I'll find something that suits your dietary requirements, then."

"Are you sure? It's dark."

"I'm the queen of darkness, remember?"

She fell back onto her arms, "Fair enough." Her eyes sparkled with relief and gratitude, "thank you, then."

I nodded and crouched over to the exit of the tent.

I wondered in the forest a few minutes before finding another lush bush of berries. I knew they were Aphrodite's favourite, so I had no doubt it was her doing that they were dotted all over the place. I used my small backpack as a container and filled it to the brim. I knew some would end up squashed against the rigid fabric, but hopefully there would be enough saved for Hanna to eat.

As I came back I noticed from afar the light in the tent, Hanna must have turned on the torch. I could see out-of-scale penis shadows drawn over the tent fabric.

I bit my lip and crawled inside.

The expression on Callisto's face as she saw me appearing was priceless. She was examining, torch in mouth, the dildo we had apparently won. The moment her eyes fell on mine the torch fell at her feet.

"Anything interesting?" I asked.

"No - I mean I don't" she scrambled to pick up the torch, pushing the toy back in her backpack. "I was just curious," she said at last.

"To see if it was worth all of this effort?" I teased her.

Callisto was definitely embarrassed now, struggling to look at me in the eyes "I think it is.. I mean it could be. Potentially. In the future. If one wanted, that is to say."

"I think it's useless," I declared instead.

"Huh?"

"My hands work just fine."

There was a second of loaded silence as her expression struggled to recompose itself.

My chest thundered.

She was so close.

"So.. what have you got?" Her voice seemed strangled.

I took the bag hanging from my shoulders and opened it. Inside there were enough berries to fill a starved belly. "Blueberries?" I asked, as my palms became sweaty.

"Wow. How did you find so many?"

"A little help from a God I guess," Aphrodite had done one good thing for all the trouble she'd caused.

I watched, tense, as Hanna stuffed her mouth with the contents of my bag. "So you believe in God, huh?" She asked in between mouthfuls.

I paused. "Kinda."

Another handful of berries disappeared into her mouth.

"I think Gods are as powerful as you make them to be," I stared at the blue smudge on her corner of her mouth. It looked delectable.

"Plural?"

"If there can be one, there can be multiple don't you think? There is no way of proving otherwise as far as you know."

"I never thought of it like this."

Her fingers were well stained with the deep blue of the fruit, too. I had a vision of licking them clean, one by one.

"If you believe the Gods will bless you and act according to their precepts, don't you think it's more likely that they'll listen to their prayers? On the other hand, if you ignore their existence why would they bother with helping you?"

She shoved yet another handful into her mouth. "Like Santa Clause."

She was so damn close to me, I could smell the blueberry scent on her breath.

"What?" I asked perplexed.

"You don't have Santa in Greece?" She asked, even more surprised than I was.

I shook my head.

"It's a mythological figure of sorts. He has a great fashion sense: he wears white and red fluffy robes with a big belt and an equally big belly." She said enthusiastically.

"And how is that the same as a God?" I asked horrified.

"He brings gifts at Christmas to all the kids who behaved well. The kids who were told of his existence behave well in order to get their presents."

"The outfit sounds ludicrous," I said, hesitating. "But the rest doesn't sound too off the mark, I'll admit."

"What do your Gods look like?" She asked, distracted. Her eyes were firmly fixed on my mouth.

"Big, strong, wise beyond what humans could possibly imagine and, of course, very attractive."

"That seems something you'd say to describe yourself."

I wiped my thumb across her bottom lip. My eyes trapped in hers "Perhaps"

"I mean you are big and strong and you know.." She said, hypnotized.

"Wise beyond what any human could imagine?"

"No, the other thing" She said.

Chapter 20
Hanna

THERE WAS A PAUSE AS Artemis, in front of me, realised what I had just said.

I can't believe I said that. Again.

My whole body was shivering, and I was pretty sure ninety percent of it was embarrassment rather than cold.

"I am so sorry, I didn't-"

And then Artemis looked at me with an expression I struggled to read. Her features morphing from sadness, to fear, to..lust?

Her stoic expression had taught me, in the short time we'd spent together, to read every wrinkle in her skin, every inch of it like a map to her emotions. But perhaps, this time, I was reading too much.

"No..it's fine" she said, but her hands were shaking.

Perhaps she felt it too, this unbearable distance between us. But maybe, just like me, she didn't know yet what stood behind the thin line of her camaraderie.

I stayed quiet and swallowed. It was all I could do. I was never brave in these matters.

"I think the same of you... it's just that I can't," she said, at last, breaking the silence.

"Is it because of, uh, Callisto?"

She nodded. I saw her shivering.

"It doesn't have to be serious you know. Perhaps we could just have fun."

Artemis looked confused."You think?"

"Of course," I said, feigning more certainty than I felt. "This doesn't have to be anymore than two women having a bit of fun."

I didn't actually believe a word of what I'd said.

Rather, I believed *her* perfectly capable of it but I knew my limits: I had never known sex without feelings.

Her eyes were on me, the hunger and desire in them reflected my own desire and my thoughts scattered. Artemis moved towards me little by little until I could see her face just an inch from mine, her breath caressing my face. Her eyes were glinting, the only light in the tent.

"I can't"

"We don't have to.. It's ok."

She was so close, I could feel the heat radiating from her body. Her skin was within my reach.

"What's scaring you?" I whispered in the dark.

You. I imagined her saying.

I drew my finger, slow and feverish, down her chest. She was a marvel, a work of art, one of the universe's wonders. Every dip and cranny, every curve of hers sliding under my fingertips, the fabric of her clothing curling up under the pressure.

Her eyes followed my touch.

I didn't know where my bravery came from and I didn't care. All I wanted was her.

Mine, I thought. And her mouth opened, warm and inviting.

I bit her lip and drank in her scent.

My back hit the hard floor. The weight of her pushing me down, her hand yanked at my shirt. She was hungry, all at once. Driven by that same desire I felt, the one I had fought back from the moment I saw her.

She hurled herself against my neck, her teeth sinking in my soft flesh.

"I am not scared" she growled.

Did she know the power she had over me?

I wrapped my legs around her, pressing against her hard body. I rubbed senselessly against her stomach, driven mad with desire.

As much as I took, she gave.

Every inch of my skin that had been touched by her mouth was seared with her signature. *Artemis*, it said. *Artemis. Artemis.*

Because I was hers.

All that had happened between us, all that had gone on until this point, was like a role-play. A play pretend where I did not belong, naked, to her world. And she to mine.

But we did. And that was false. And we were lying.

When her moan filled my ears, my nails left trails on her skin.

I gasped. "Please."

I grip her hair. I wanted to taste her again.

But when our eyes crossed, it was as if a crystal glass has broken and Artemis had realised I wasn't who she thought I was. At once, the spell was broken.

I tried to pull myself up on my elbows while Artemis pushed herself up and away from me.

My heart was beating furiously and I was suddenly aware of how naked I was without her eyes on me.

Her pose was defensive.

"Did I do something wrong?" I asked, panicked. I pushed my bras' straps back in place.

It looked as if there were tears swelling in her eyes, but it was so dark that I couldn't be entirely sure.

I wanted to tell her that I wouldn't hurt her, that she shouldn't be fearful, that I respected her pain and would give her any space she needed.

I wanted to hold her and kiss her.

I wanted to whisper "It's going to be fine."

But she was gone and I couldn't cross the wall that now stood between us. I was left alone with the path her fingers traced on me still seared onto my skin, my breathing still ragged. I felt the cold harsh reality of rejection hit me like an icy wind.

Still, I put a hand towards her. "Artemis?"

No answer.

I pulled my hand away, put on my shirt, and exited the tent.

The sky above me brimmed with stars.

Chapter 21
Artemis

CALLISTO'S SMELL HUNG in the heavy air of the tent, swirling around me like an emotional whirlwind.

"Now what?" Callisto asked, her face was hidden in the hollow of my neck. She was so sweet against the bitterness pooling inside me.

Father's thunderous laugh was still echoing inside my head - turn a nymph into a Goddess? Are you kidding, Artemis?- that's what he had dared to say.

I clenched my fists. "There must be another way that I haven't considered. Someone who knows, a potion, perhaps a centaur who has the answers we're looking for-"

"Love" Callisto's hand pulled me to face her. "It's ok."

"It's not ok. He disrespected you. He laughed at us." I tried to steady my breath. "He treated us as if it was a joke."

"This is not about your Father, Artemis." Her eyes glinted against mine, "what are you afraid of?"

I took another steadying breath. Another surge of panic threatened to overwhelm me, like a rogue wave on the horizon. I had a bad feeling. Something was going to happen to her. I felt it. "What if we can't be together any longer?"

"What do you mean?"

"I can't lose you."

"Artemis," Callisto's soothing smile was still firmly in place. "I love you and we have an eternity ahead of us."

"You promise?"

"I promise." she said "Until the end of times. I'm not going anywhere."

I shook the memory off.

The woman that had been in my arms until a moment before was not Callisto.

She was her own person, a human. Hanna.

And perhaps, just maybe, I liked the way she was. It was her fierce nature, her optimism, her ability to react so well under stress, to take a situation in her hand.

I liked it.

But the realisation had come with a fact: Callisto, as I knew her, was gone. I would never again have a chance to experience her body holding onto mine, or hear her laugh.

Nostalgia hit me, but in a way I had not expected it: it wasn't yelling in my chest, as if attempting to shatter my heart's walls like glass, but rather like the gentle hum of a long-forgotten song. I had tried to mask it for a long time, but Callisto had gone and I must be ready to accept it. Not quite tonight, perhaps, as I digested it all, but tomorrow. Tomorrow seemed great, if I could find a way for Hanna to forgive me.

"I am sorry," I rehearsed quietly in the tent. I was not used to using those words. They came out stilted. But Hanna was kind and understanding, certainly she would forgive me.

I head towards the tent's exit. It was going to be fine.

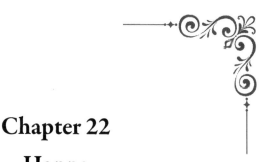

Chapter 22
Hanna

IT WASN'T GOING TO be fine.

And, while I usually disliked it, right now I appreciated the cold. There was something about icy air and a star dotted skies that woke my senses. The situation was suddenly very clear to me: Artemis was not into me. Or at least not as much as I was into her.

And here was the undeniable proof of it: there was no way I could have stopped. Despite being far from a one-night-stand type, despite my promise of keeping away, I could have not denied Artemis anything she'd wanted just now.

Which was a huge mistake. Huge. I didn't even know how I was going to tell Lori about it.

But maybe Lori didn't need to know, because nothing had really happened, and nothing needed to happen anyway.

One thing was for sure, though: I was fully pathetic for trying to make it work with someone who was so clearly not into me. And I was damn sure not to let those gorgeous eyes trick me one more time.

Just as I made my resolution, Artemis crawled out of the tent with a sheepish smile on her face. It looked adorable on her.

Wishful thinking. I reminded myself and smiled back tensely.

"I wanted to-"

"Look," I interrupted, "I completely understand what happened before and there's no reason to give any long winded explanation."

I certainly didn't want to hear any version of *I am just not that into you.*

"Really, you do?"

"Yes," I looked into her hazel eyes and reminded myself that the tenderness in them was really a self-sabotaging product of my imagination, "We're good."

"I just wanted to-"

"Look, it's already damn embarrassing as is, talking about it would only make it worse."

The heat of shame was burning bright on my face and my stomach was in knots. "Nothing happened tonight, ok?"

She seemed confused for a second and then nodded, "as you wish," she said.

I headed back into our tiny tent and rolled the towel I had in my bag into a circular shape for my pillow. My old Dad had showed me that trick.

I heard her come in shortly after. She was silent and unmoving for a few minutes. I felt a shiver down my spine at the thought of the embarrassment I'd caused to myself.

"Would you rather me sleep outside?" She asked.

"Of course not," I replied, adjusting inside the sleeping bag. "The tent is spacious enough for two, and I don't have any more right to it than you do."

"It was in your bag."

"And we are teammates, aren't we?" I asked. I hoped my face was arranged in a way that conveyed the concept of partnership that I intended.

"We are," she whispered.

I lay back down and attempted to fall back asleep.

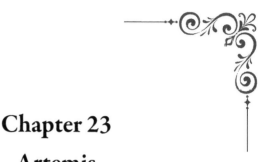

Chapter 23

Artemis

IT WAS CLEAR THAT HANNA was not sleeping. The rise and slump of her shoulders was irregular, and by experience I knew she was a snorer: tonight I could not hear her.

I decided to gather more berries rather than waste time stewing in the tent. Despite the events of the evening, I felt a rush of excitement as I discovered some plump strawberries in one of the most dense parts of the vegetation: Hanna would certainly appreciate them. Not that my excursion was driven by the desire to be forgiven for my jerk reaction. Even though I'll admit, I thought the gesture might double as an un-said apology.

No, my main concern was for her health. Aphrodite's behaviour was almost criminal in it's thoughtlessness. Didn't she know humans could not survive very long without food?

I was back a few hours later, with another rucksack full of berries and heard the stirring that pre announced Hanna's awakening.

For the rest of the morning, as we packed up the tent and searched, again, for our way home, I was very aware of the dark smudges under her eyes, and the slower rhythm she kept.

"Perhaps you'd prefer me to carry you?" I suggested.

She gave me a smile that didn't reach her eyes "There's no need, I'm good. Thank you."

I had this growing desire in me to make her laugh. She had been the entertainer, the chit chatter and the happy ray of sunshine in every situation both when I was around and not, so her growing silence, stained by the visible effort it cost her to keep going, was unsettling.

"Hey, look," I said halting in the road. I crouched down few steps ahead of her and picked up the tiny snail there, so minuscule it was barely visible. I gently moved the poor creature further from the path into the long grass.

As I returned, Hanna looked at me surprised, "I thought you hunted animals, not helped them."

"I hunt for food. I wouldn't hunt an animal if not to consume it. That's cruel."

An indecisive look hung on her face. "that was kind of you," and then her eyes traveled toward the snail, who was leaving a slow slippery trail behind. "I am glad she's safe now in her little house."

She looked at me with a genuine smile and I realised how much I had missed it. I scanned the woods nearby for another wounded animal to rescue.

And then I heard them. The voices. Indistinctly coming our way. Nerea's powerful call was clear amongst them.

I doubted Hanna could hear them yet, "I think we're close."

"Really?"

Then she heard them too. Suddenly forgetting her tiredness, she rushed towards the sound, " Lori, Lori!" She screamed in their direction.

The voice of her human friend shrieked back our names.

Hanna turned toward me with the biggest smile, even brighter than the last, "they're here! They found us!"

"Looks like it," I said, attempting to match her excitement about the unexpected turn of events.

Oh Nerea, I hope you're prepared for what's coming.

Chapter 24

Hanna

WHEN I SAW LORI, I could not resist jumping into her arms.

"I was so damn worried," she said. Her tone was almost angry, so much so that I was afraid she was about to go off on me.

I held her tighter.

"I thought you were being eaten by fishes, or neck-snapped in a ditch," she lowered her voice "Or maybe someone had disposed of you."

She shot a side-eye to Artemis.

"I'm fine. Hey," I grabbed her on either side of her head, "look at me. I'm fine." I didn't want my best friend to go off on Artemis, of all people. Judging by her muscles, my friend would easily be snapped in two.

"So what happened?" She asked.

"I'll tell you everything but first we need to go back and I need to swallow a week's worth of food."

"Oh, wait," her hand dug into her backpack for a bit until she produced what looked like a cheese sandwich, "I got this for you."

I was so happy to see food, I snatched the sandwich from her hand. I peeled the plastic off so fast it ripped and, without hesitation, shoved the sandwich as far into my mouth as it would fit. It was only then that I realised how terribly impolite I had been. I turned around.

"Sorry, I ate some, but I've taken out the bits around my bite with my hands," I showed Artemis the crumbs laying in my palm. "Sorry" I said again.

"No need. I'm not hungry"

I looked at her in shock.

"Really, I am not trying to be heroic. I just lost my appetite."

I thought of last night. Perhaps she meant what had happened had been so disgusting..?

I let the words hang in the air, before going back to my place next to Lori.

"She didn't want it?"

I shook my head. I was still thinking of her words. Was I responsible for the loss of appetite?

"Better, more for you" Lori said with a smile.

I swallowed the rest of the sandwich in two big mouthfuls and took a deep breath. "Oh God, I cannot wait to be back in the tent, I miss my sleeping bag."

"We didn't walk that far actually, so I am surprised you didn't make it home last night."

"We walked sooooo far Lori. Close to ten hours yesterday. We must have gone in circle without realising it."

"That's exactly what must have happened" Artemis voice said behind me. There was an edge to it. I turned around and saw her walking side by side with Nerea. The latter's expression was dark, far from the relaxed stoney yoga teacher I had come to know.

I made no further comment and walked ahead holding onto Lori's arm.

"SO, WHAT HAPPENED?" Lori asked again. "And before you say anything, let me specify that I am not buying the story that you walked in circles for ten hours. It's literally a straight path." She was perched on my stool. Artemis was nowhere in sight, though the last time I'd seen her, she'd been asking Nerea for a word. They'd probably gone somewhere to talk and judging by Artemis murderous expression, it wasn't the pleasant kind.

"Lori, I swear to you we followed the path and, somehow, despite all of the walking, it led us nowhere."

"You sure you don't want to change your version? I'll give you another chance," she said with a raised brow.

I was offended that she wouldn't believe me, but, in truth, I wouldn't have believed my version either.

I took her hands in mine, and leaned forward "Lori, you have to believe me. I wouldn't lie to you."

She looked straight into my eyes. "Ok, I believe you," she declared at last. "But that means it was that asshole of a woman who played a trick on you."

"No, she didn't, she seemed just as frustrated as I was," I said.

"Babe, I love you, but you are so damn naive." Lori shook her head in disbelief.

"I can't really argue with that," I said, pushing my bag out of the way, and scooting closer. "But I'm right about this one."

Keeping secrets from Lori had not panned out that well so far.

"Lori, there is something I need to tell you." I said lowering my voice. "Something did happen with her."

Lori's hands flew to her mouth "No, you didn't."

"Yes, I did. Well, not exactly. I mean, I don't think it counts."

Heavy lines of shock were drawn on Lori's face, to the point that I was afraid her features would be permanently stuck in her surprised expression.

"Ok, ok, let me explain."

"You better explain! What the hell do you mean?"

"I'm trying!"

She sat back in her intent-listening pose, "shoot."

"Ok so, first...."

WHEN I'D FINISHED THE story I could tell Lori was more shocked than at the beginning, "so she just pushed you away?"

"Yeah, I think perhaps I misread it and she wasn't much into it. You know how sometimes you think you're in the mood, and then oops, you're not anymore?"

Lori gave me a thorough look, "I mean it seems unlikely after what you told me."

"I know but what other explanation do you have for it?"

"Maybe she's not ready to move on from her ex?" She said. "Not that it makes it any better, really. If anything, in my mind, she's just moved from the asshole category to the idiot one. She could have had a piece of that sweet sexy ass of yours and instead she decided to screw it up." She grabbed my hand and looked straight in my eyes "Whatever's going through her head, it is not you, I guarantee it."

"Of course you'd say that, you're my friend," I argued back.

"And that's exactly why I am your friend."

"Because I have a nice piece of ass?" I raised a brow and offered a smile.

"No, idiot. It's because you are sweet."

Chapter 25
Artemis

As we reached the edge of the meadow, I turned toward Nerea. "A word."

She nodded and followed me quietly into the main tent.

"Before you say anything Artemis, there was a mistake I didn't-"

She didn't get the chance to finish the sentence. My hand flew to the collar of her vest, holding Nerea high above the ground. Her feet were dangling useless underneath her, and her face was a mask of fear.

The group of nymphs lounging on the surrounding sofas fled at once.

"This has stopped being funny" I could feel my eyes burning in anger, and my muscles swirl with the desire to hit her. I would never do that to one of my nymphs, though: I did not care to ensure loyalty with violence.

"Eusachia didn't tell me this was going to happen, I had no clue," she said as I pulled her closer to me.

"Why did you think she would tell you? Are you buddies now?"

"No," she squeezed her eyes.

I let go of my grip on her collar and watched her retreat into the corner.

"You're supposed to check on her, go behind her back, make a truce to, do whatever you have to to make it all a bit more bearable for me." I took a deep breath before continuing, "I thought this was just your funny way of trying to push Hanna and I together. To force me to acknowledge it was time to move on from Callisto, but what you've done..."

I turned towards her in a flair of fury, "you could have killed her, had this little fun idea of hers gone on any longer. Don't you realise how delicate humans are?"

"I never thought Aphrodite would let her get hurt, that wasn't the point she was trying to make!"

"Wasn't the point?" My voice thundered through the tent. "My sister lacks basic practicality. She is vain and self centred. How could you put the life of Hanna in the hands of such a superficial creature?"

I grabbed the blade of a knife nearby and hurled it against the white scoreboard on the corner. It landed right in the centre, on the line dividing the tally of points for each player.

"My queen," she cautioned.

I gripped my right hand, with a sharp ache sizzling through it. I looked down to see the blood falling in a crimson stream, dripping down my wrist and finally landing on the grass underneath. One drop at a time.

I stared at it, in shock. Then looked at Nerea.

"How could..?" I felt my hands shaking. It was impossible. I couldn't bleed. I was a Goddess: indestructible, unwoundable, untouchable. "My queen, come here. Let me help." I saw the same fear I felt mirrored in her eyes.

She tore a piece of her clothing and wrapped it around my arm. She was quick with the bandaging and knotted it tightly around my wrist.

"I don't understand" I said, again, staring into the distance. My thoughts were scattered.

How could it be? "Do you think my sister could cheat?"

"I don't think she'd be capable of it."

"As if you knew what my sister was capable of," I scoffed bitterly, feeling the throb of the wound underneath the fabric of the bandages.

"I think it might be -" She quieted suddenly.

"Oh, now you've lost your tongue, Nerea?" I asked in anger.

"No, my queen," she hesitated, " I think this might be a sign that you are losing your bet."

The alarm I felt at her words, shook me to my core, "you mean I'm human now?" Even I could detect the shakiness of my voice.

"Not yet, I don't think. You're still quite strong despite the prolonged lack of food," she observed.

I thought back to the previous night. I had felt something akin to affection for Hanna, had I not? It hadn't been simple admiration or camaraderie.

"Did something happened between the two of you?" Nerea asked.

"A kiss."

That's how Aphrodite had decided to trigger the bet.

"You're sure, my queen?"

"You're doubting my memory?"

"According to the contract - the one you didn't want to read because you'd win no matter what- it's only sex that could lead to a loss of powers."

"That's not exactly what happened..."

Now I knew: sex with Hanna would condemn me for the next eight years. Eighty years in a God's time were of no significance, but as a human, I'd experience time at the same snail paced the rest of humanity did. I'd be subject to disease, physical pain, and if my sister had any choice in it, probably several amputations. "So there is still a way to get untangled from this mess."

"That's my hope, my queen."

"Bring me back the knife," I said at once.

"What do you intend to do with it?"

"I'm going to bleed to death, and come to the end of my human life and then reappear back on the Olympus," I said.

"Would it really be so hard to keep this feeling from growing, my queen?" She wasn't teasing me but rather genuinely inquiring about the seriousness of my intentions.

The knife disappeared into thin air. "That wouldn't work, my queen. There's a clause in the contract that requires you to live as a human for seventy years minimum. So you wouldn't actually die, you'd just reappear on this same floor but with blood to account for with the rest of the campers. Also, I thought you wanted to beat your sister?"

"And you wouldn't lie to me about the terms, right, Nerea?"

"Of course not, the contract was forged by Athena herself."

I moved towards the closest chair, and plopped down on it, "there is little hope at this point isn't there?" I said.

"Well, it depends on how your sisters are doing, my queen."

"Any news from tham?" I asked, a new spark of hope lighting within me.

Nerea gave me a smirk. "Not any better than you, my queen."

"So not everything is lost."

"Not at all," she said, "I'd dare say that if the two of them become human again, it would be quite easy for you to strike a new deal so you could all go back to the Olympus safe and sound."

I reflected on her words.

I caught the look in Nerea's eyes, "don't think you're forgiven quite yet!" I warned, struggling to keep the tone as stern as I wished.

"Of course not, my queen."

"Good."

She was looking down towards the floor, seemingly contrite, "I would like to specify though that this was a difficult information to retrieve, so it possibly earns me a partial forgiveness?"

"What? Did you have to sleep with that pain in the ass Eusachia to get it? Because only that sacrifice would ease my anger toward your betrayal."

There was a moment of silence from Nerea.

I turned towards her in shock "You didn't?!?"

"You said I had to play dirty!" She said with a faint voice.

"And I am sure it was a huge hardship..." I commented.

"I mean I wouldn't exactly call it that-"

Then she took another look at my expression "- it was the worst experience of my existence," she concluded hastily.

"Thought so." I said. "And by the way, show me to some good food. I'm starving and the sight of blood is not helping."

"Of course, my queen," she said before scurrying away.

THERE WAS AN UNNATURAL silence at dinner.

The rattling of forks on plates was louder than any whispered chit chat around the table. I knew what they were all thinking, of course: a wounded goddess. Unprecedented.

"They are all looking at me, Nerea."

There was one particular set of eyes I was concerned about. Hanna's. I disliked her seeing me in such a state. Hell, I disliked all of them seeing in such a state. But with Hanna I had a particular interest in looking as tough and strong as I could.

"I think we have bigger troubles, my queen," Nerea said, leaning towards me.

"What?" I asked, my tone biting from the pain and fatigue.

"I think the situation might be more dangerous than you think."

"How come?"

"Let's just say you haven't always been the kindest with Aphrodite's ladies. I think them seeing you like this, vulnerable might inspire... revenge."

"Sure, I might have broken a few of their toiletries on occasion but I don't think I've ever truly hurt them."

"You cursed not one but two of them to eternal crow's feet around their eyes."

"Ohhh yeah, no, I did do that."

"Exactly. And they are the vengeful kind."

I looked around and saw their elaborate hairstyles and their fine clothing. They were my sister's nymphs. They shared millennia at her command. I had no reason to doubt any of their capabilities.

"Still, they can't kill me right? " I said, my mind running to the worst possible scenario.

"I think they could do worse than that if they wanted to."

"Nerea, why are you telling me this?"

"Because you've got to be careful. So far you thought losing a bet was the worse case scenario, I think now things have become more risky."

I swallowed a bite of meat, "why are you warning me about this, Nerea? Have I not been brutal with you as well, on occasions?"

"My queen, you've definitely been challenging at times, but there's nothing that could persuade me to go from serving you to serving Aphrodite. She is... well, unkind is an understatement."

"So it's not loyalty to me that keeps you with me but the fear of the alternative."

She looked at me sideways, "perhaps if you could be more gentle on occasions... there wouldn't be a reason for me to think in such terms." She cleaned her mouth with her white napkin and pushed it to the side. "I'm on your side, my queen, mostly because I am afraid of what would happen at the end of seventy years."

"Fear suits me better. Thank you, Nerea."

"You're welcome."

I threw a look at Hanna. If I was in danger, she was too.

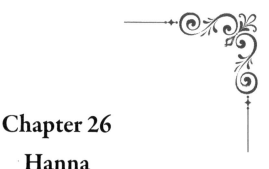

Chapter 26
Hanna

DESPITE MY BETTER JUDGEMENT, I continued throwing worried glances at Artemis. Her hand was wrapped in a blood-stained bandage and the little devil on my shoulder kept urging me to go talk to her to check she was ok. I knew, though, she wouldn't appreciate public fussing.

After pudding, I thought.

But before the end of dinner, Eusachia raised her glass.

"I would like you all to join me in raising a glass to Hanna and Artemis. They've had a rough couple of days and we couldn't be more relieved to have them back with us safe and sound."

Artemis' face was a perfect mask of stone while the group of women raised their glasses.

"To celebrate their return, " she continued, "we have decided to organise a special bonfire.."

"Marshmallow time, finally!" Lori whispered in my ear. "I almost wish you had gotten lost sooner."

I threw a badly-aimed punch at her arm.

"I'm kidding, I'm kidding"

"...You're free for half an hour until the celebration starts in the middle of the meadows. And once more, welcome back home, Hanna and Artemis."

"I'm going to help them set up the fire," Lori said enthusiastically, before dashing out of the tent after Eusachia.

The other's left the tent slowly. Artemis was one of the last to leave. Her eyes met mine before Nerea escorted her out.

I was going to meet her at the tent. I really wanted to make sure the cut was clean and not at risk of infections. Not to mention, ask her how in the hell it had happened.

"Oh Hanna, here you are!" Loelia stomped in front of me, hovering over to me on some make-shift crutches. "Just the person I wanted to talk to."

Her foot was bent almost ninety degrees more left than it should. "Oh God." I looked at it in horror, what the hell was happening around here that so many people were injured? "What happened to you?"

"Well.. there was a little accident with Eusachia earlier in the week."

Another violent image of our campsite manager, this time snapping a leg in two, popped into my brain, "Was it hiking?"

"Sort of.."

"Have you had a doctor look at it?" How was this woman not writhing in pain?!

She waved her hand. "It's not as bad as it looks."

If she said so.

"I actually was hoping to talk to you.."

"If it is about the leg.. I am a vet. I am not qualified to patch up human injuries..-"

"No, that's not it at all." She shook her head. "..I wanted to apologise. About how I treated you before."

Leolia's face was the very portrait of sorrow. "These last couple of days we've been so worried about you and Artemis, that it made me realise just how unfair I was towards you."

"You weren't."

"I was. I may have developed a bit of a crush on Artemis and the fact that she was paying so much attention to you, made me act a bit..crazy."

That made both of us. I could empathise with the queen of darkness turning one delusional.

I extended a hand. "We're good, Loelia. Don't worry about it."

She shook my hand, perched on one of the crutches. "Thank you...one more thing," she readjusted her weight across the two branches, "I don't wish to hold you back any longer but... there is something weird on my wound which I cannot make sense of."

"I thought it wasn't as bad as it looked."

She looked distraught, " I mean it's barely hurting now, it's just that I am a bit of a hypochondriac you see and..."

I threw one last glance at Artemis striding towards the tent. She could wait a couple of minutes.

"Well then," I smiled, "let's see what's going on."

"You've been so very kind with me," she said, as she hopped toward the tent.

"It's not an issue at all," I said, reassuring her.

She pushed her head on my shoulder, "oh you are so dear."

I retreated slightly with an uncomfortable feeling rolling in my stomach.

"Watch your head," I said as we crossed the threshold of the tent.

I made Loelia lie on the ground and unpeeled the bandage on her wound carefully so as not to twist the foot further. Everything looked in order. The cut was still not completely healed, but it showed good progress, exceptional progress, really.

"It's all in order, here," I said, "but you need to see a doctor. That ankle looks.. bad, really bad."

"Thank you, you've been so kind"

"There's no need to thank me, really." I said, with an awkward pat on her back. "I was happy to help. But I do have another unlucky camper to see to, if you're ok now."

"Wait," she said, "I have a great bottle from the winery that Eusachia gifted me. Care to share?"

"I don't handle wine very well..."

"Oh but this is not just good wine. It's a 50 years old bottle of deliciousness."

"50?!" I said. "It must be worth a lot."

"Oh it is. Let me share it with you, in exchange for your kindness."

"It's not necessary, really."

"I insist, plus it is a gift, so it has cost me nothing," she said as she forced the bottle cap open with her bare hands. Not even a cork screw for this woman.

"Well, Eusachia must be feeling really sorry about your accident," I said with a smile. "I didn't get any bottle of wine."

"When I said gift, I meant the involuntary kind," Loelia said with a wink.

Before I could protest drinking stolen wine, Loelia passed me one of the glasses she had conjured from her bag. "Let's cheer to your kind heart," she said pouring out us both generous measures of the merlot coloured liquid.

A little voice in my head suggested I put down the glass and leave the tent but I pushed it away. Leolia was being friendly.

I brought the crystal glass to my mouth and swallowed a few sips.

"Wow," I said "This is..."

"Straight out of heaven?" She said smiling.

"That's a good way to describe it," I looked at the glass. The colour was vibrant and the taste sweeter than any wine I had ever tasted. As if the grapes had been soaked in honey.

I finished the rest in one big gulp.

"More?" She asked.

"No, that's quite enough. I have very low tolerance for wine," I said, rising unsteadily to my feet. The world was a bit shaky. Wasn't it too soon for that?

"You're going to leave me here all alone to finish this?" She asked with a pout.

"I really need to go," I said, gripping at the pole holding the tent in place.

"If you change your mind.." came her voice from behind me.

My head was pounding. I tried to take a few steps but my legs were not cooperating. Damn, I should remind myself to never ever drink a 50 years old bottle of Merlot, or whatever the name of that wine was, again.

The fire outside seemed to rise high in the sky. The contour of the flaming tongues, bright against the tent fabric, was dancing in front of my eyes. "The f-.." I said.

My tongue was glued in my mouth, unable to move.

"Shh.." Came Loelia's soft voice.

Help, I tried to scream.

But she was on me, her crutches forgotten nearby. I tried to push forward, but my legs gave in.

My back hit the ground and the world went black.

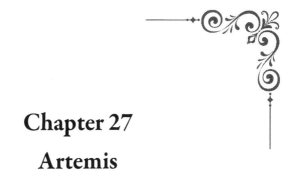

Chapter 27
Artemis

I WAITED A FEW MINUTES for Hanna to reappear at the door. There was a growing sense of unease in my stomach, that I could not make sense of. Outside I could hear Aphrodite's ladies chanting around the bonfire and I wondered what Hanna and Lori thought of all the commotion.

Half an hour later, I'd had enough of pacing around the tent.

I went out into the meadow to find the bonfire celebration in full swing. It was a striking sight: Eusachia was kneeled at its base chanting her prayers to my sister while the rest of the nymphs were pirouetting around her, holding their long white dresses, their hair dancing in wild, tangled streams.

Hanna was not there, though.

I scanned nearby. Nothing.

Maybe I had lost my sight too. I could have asked Nerea, but I was not sure whether I still trusted her.

There was only one thing to do: Hanna's friend. Lori had joined the worship and there was no way of telling how much alcohol it had taken to get her to sway her hips to the flames. Still, I had to try.

"Hey." I tapped on her shoulder. "I need your help."

Her hips drew one last eight before her eyes settle on me. "Oh, Miss. Broody Butch. There she is."

The rest of the nymphs, mad with euphoria, did not seem to notice my intrusion.

"I need your help," I said again, making sure to enunciate each word.

The chanting grew in volume. "What?"

"I need your help. It's Hanna. I can't find her."

She nodded her head towards the woods and set off with me trailing behind her. "Why are you looking for her? To make her feel bad again?"

"I'm just worried."

"Worried that she's gone to have fun with someone else?"

"No.. I have this feeling that something's off."

"She's probably just somewhere drinking wine. You've been really shitty to her non-stop, no wonder she wants to let off some steam, far away from you."

"You reckon she's dancing somewhere, too?"

"Hey! I don't like your air of superiority when you said *dancing*. I was 2005 Fancy Feet's Most Promising Cha Cha Dancer, thank you very much."

"My apologies, it was not my intention to insult such an obvious talent."

"Good."

"Any idea where she could be?"

"Were you looking for me?" We both turned toward her at once.

Hanna's hair was no longer in a hastily arranged bun, but fell loose on her shoulders. A light coat of makeup covered her eyes and lips, the rouge on her mouth made her eyes sparkle even brighter.

I was enchanted.

"What's all this? I never see you wear make up," Lori said.

"At times it's necessary," she said in a soft honey-like tone. She winked at me.

"You know what? You're right, babe. Girl power!"

Hanna ignored her. "I thought maybe you'd like to talk alone, in the tent. With me," she said, sliding her fingers down my arm, swaying slightly.

"Hanna, I think you've had quite a bit to drink.. perhaps we can stand by the fire. Chit chat for a bit," Lori said, seeming disturbed.

Hanna's eyes flashed with irritation, only for an instant. "Lori, I'd rather go with her, if that's ok. Thank you, though."

I smiled at her. "I'll get wine for us, then."

"Let me take care of that," Hanna insisted, raising the empty glass of wine in her hand.

I leaned in towards her. "Thank you," I whispered.

She giggled and left, swaying her hips left and right in a way that struck me as vaguely familiar.

Once she was out of earshot I turned towards Hanna's human friend. "Is that normal?" I asked.

"Hey! You don't have the right to go around and drink-shame my friend."

I could tell that In her effort to defend her friend, Lori was purposely glossing over the weirdness happening in front of her.

"So you've seen her before like this?"

"Pfff. All the time. My friend is a panty-dropper. I'm just going to check on her, though. You know, to make sure she won't make all of the women in the camp fall at her knees...".

"Wait a second. Before you go," I stopped her. "Do you know where she went after dinner?"

"I left before her.. I think I saw her talk to Loelia, though."

My fist clenched. "I'll go talk to Hanna. Leave it to me."

This time it was Lori's tiny figure that obstructed my way. "Nah-ah. She is my friend."

"Please. I promise to behave" Lori must have seen something in my expression, because her mouth curved into a regretful smile "Don't you dare touch her. She's way too drunk to give consent for anything."

"I know."

"Ohh..ok. Promise, though."

I looked at Lori and spoke the truth, "I can't hurt her."

The woman nodded "I still don't trust you with anything else, though.."

I could barely hear her: I was already running towards Loelia's tent as fast as I could, my feet barely touching the ground. If it was too late...

If that nymph had dared to lay a fucking finger on her...

My entire body hummed with anger.

I tore open the entrance.

And there I found her. Hanna was laying on the ground, perfectly still with her eyes closed.

Not a sound came from her, not a snore, nor a breath.

"Artemis-"

My hands wrapped against the fake-Hanna's neck, squeezing. She was still holding the bottle of wine.

The ruby liquid soaked the grass nearby.

Her eyes bulged "Pl-"

I did not care for her pleading. My grip tightened.

"Artemis."

I stopped. It was Hanna talking.

I let go at once and Loelia fell on the ground, like a puppet who's wires had been cut.

"I'm here." I kneeled at her side.

"Artemis!"

She opened her eyes and I recognised her. Her hand came down, strong and swift against my cheek.

Callisto.

Chapter 28
Callisto

MY EYES FLUTTERED OPEN.

A screeching sound had jolted me awake. Two blurred figures stood near my head, one of them floating above the ground.

That screeching sound again.

I focused on the dark stain I could see. A tattoo.

"Artemis."

I couldn't move. One of the figures turned.

"I'm here."

What was she doing in the afterworld? Was it really her?

"Artemis!" I repeated again, my voice was stronger.

And finally my vision cleared and I saw her distinctly. Her chocolate eyes, worried and tender, like they had been in Eleusis.

I'd waited for this moment for far too long.

My hand made contact with her cheek before I could make a good argument against it. The slap resonated across the tent.

"How could you?" I hissed "How, in the name of everything that's good, could you do that?"

Artemis stood petrified. Far from the temible Goddess I had known, she resembled a dog caught in the middle of stealing food.

"Callisto.." She repeated again.

"Do you have anything to say for yourself?"

Not a sound.

"Good. Because I have something to say." I tried to sit up but the room spun around me.

She held me. I had thought of those arms, every night before falling asleep. I'd dreamt of them holding me and lulling me into sleep in the wet coldness of Hades. But now the embrace was unwelcome.

"I spent the past two millennials in the afterworld hearing about the story of the cheating nymph who got punished by the Great Goddess." I clenched my jaw, "and I want a damn explanation."

"You were in the afterworld? But you can't die.. that can't be true."

"I wasn't dead." I waved my hand. She wasn't getting it. "Persephone wanted archery lessons so Hades told me I could stay."

"That's how you beat me last week...."

Hades help me. I was about to scream. "Is this the first thing you say to me?!?"

Artemis stood quiet in shellshock. "No..no..of course not."

"Then what do you have to say for yourself, eh? What was going through your mind, when you decided to call me a cheating liar?"

"I-"

"Answer me, Artemis. Now."

The Goddess looked like she was about to faint. Or cry, maybe.

"I'm sorry."

"I can't hear you."

"I am sorry." She said, moving further from me "I didn't know how to process it.. I couldn't bear the thought of you and him."

"There was no he and I! And you know it."

"Please..."

"He stole your form. He came to me looking like you. He tricked me."

"Please, stop."

"No, I won't let you run away from this anymore."

"I can't hear this. I can't. Please." She was curled up on the floor with her hands covering her ears.

"He took me against my will. He knew I would never commit such an atrocity. I was destroyed. But, you know, you accusing me of cheating on you for two millennia was the worst of it. Your betrayal hurt me more than his actions ever did."

I fell quiet.

Artemis' eyes were fixed on a spot in the distance. She looked defeated. It pained me beyond words to see her like this.

"Artemis, I know it hurts," I took her hands in mine, "but I needed you by my side then. I needed you to believe me."

Her eyes, glossy with tears, darted back to me.

My Goddess. "Artemis-"

"I tried to kill him"

"What?"

"I promised I'd take revenge on anyone who hurt you, but I just..couldn't. I couldn't do anything against him." Her head hung low, her soft sobs filled the tents.

"Why are you telling me this?"

"Because you must know I sought revenge for your pain." Artemis was shaking, lines of tears streaked down her face. "I wanted to help you, so desperately. I dreamed of it everytime Helios rode the golden chariot back, in the pitch black for a thousand nights. I'd dream of dragging a knife to His heart and ending his existence. I studied every chance, every moment. There were none."

I touched her hair, delicately, "and what good would revenge do, if you were determined to hate me, Artemis?"

She looked at me at once, her features pain with fear. Was the untamable Goddess, at last, scared of a half-dead nymph? Or was it my hatred she feared?

"Do you think I resent you for not avenging me?" I asked her.

"I'm sorry I couldn't."

I caressed her hair "What are you apologising to me for, now, Artemis?"

She clenched her fist, her eyes trapped on the ground, far away from mine "It was my fault."

I stilled my hand "What happened was not your fault. It wasn't mine either."

"It was my fault. I was greedy. We could have had forever together if only I'd never suggested we spoke to Him. Had I never given Him a chance to laugh at our dreams. I threw it all away for nothing."

I grabbed her chin, gently, "It really wasn't for nothing, love."

Her eyes, at last, turned to meet mine. "I don't need you to lie to me. I brought you in His presence. He noticed you because of me."

"You wanted to protect me, Artemis," I said, wiping the tears off her face. "You didn't want anyone to hurt me. You trusted him."

"I shouldn't have, I shouldn't."

"What he did...it's on him, love. Only on him."

She gripped my garments. "Please, forgive me."

"I can't absolve you from your pain, Artemis. It's you who is causing it."

It was then that she understood. Perhaps she read the forgiveness in my eyes, perhaps it was her own she accepted. But at once, the divine Huntress fell apart, slumped on the ground, she wept properly now. The Earth shook under her pain for the first time in two thousand years.

I welcomed her into my arms. "It's ok, Artemis. Shh, it's fine."

I let her weep until her breathing was calm. The sobs quieted and even then, I did not stop caressing her hair. How long had she been in need of this?

"Forgive me, please," she said, at last. "I was quicker to hate Him than I was to love you, once you were gone. I shouldn't have behaved the way I did. I regret it now."

"For the only apology you do owe me, love, I forgive you."

With her eyes dried, she sat back down."How much time do we have?"

"Forever" I gestured at my clothes, the tent "I'm here."

"No I mean, back again, on Earth.."

"Forever."

She looked at me as if I had lost my mind.

Couldn't she see?

"She is me and I am her, Artemis. Hanna lives in a world that's 2000 years older and holds relatively few memories. She lives in a world that is far more equal than the one we've existed in. She is my young, feistier version. I am her wise one with rotten memories. We share one soul. If she were to live as I had, for as long as I did, she would be me. The Gods account for our nature, our existence accounts for our nurture."

"Are you saying that once you wake up as her, you'll never get your memories of us, back?"

"That's the wrong question, love."

"What's the right one, then?"

"Could you love me again and again, in a world that changes and holds no memories? Is our love, as you promised me the day we exchanged our vows, unweathered by changes coming in its way?"

"You don't know what you're asking me to do."

"I suspect I understand it better than you do." I smiled, "you were always the most stubborn of the Goddesses."

"But I can't let go of them, the memories." Her face was crumpled with fresh pain.

"Nobody will ever take them from you, love, I am the one with the curse, damned to come back again and again as a human. You'll have to hold the fort for us both."

"You know me..." She looked at me, forlorn, "I need you."

"I know, love, and I'll always be with you, in some form or another, I'll always come back."

Artemis' head bowed forward.

"Hey, look at me."

Her eyes met mine "It's going to be ok. Really."

The shadow of a hopeful smile played over her mouth.

"The savage, untamable Goddess in need of a human nymph. If your sister could hear you.."

"She probably can."

"Then tell her I say hi."

"Will you be alright?" She asked me. "Being a human is not ideal, is it?"

"Well, it's true I'm always hungry and tired and there is always some part of me that aches. I can't imagine what being seventy will feel like."

"It sounds atrocious. I don't want it for you."

"There's worse in life," I shrugged and smirked her way.

All of a sudden a great tiredness fell over me.

She searched my eyes "Is this when you say goodbye?" She asked.

"Until our next life together."

"What if I can't? What if I can't do it?" She was growing agitated just as my heart filled with peace.

"Then I'll wish you the best from the afterworld, in between lives."

"You promise?"

I was struggling to keep my eyes open, fighting the abyss, because she needed to know. "I love you, Artemis. Now and always. Whatever comes our way."

I felt her arms against me and then the world went black.

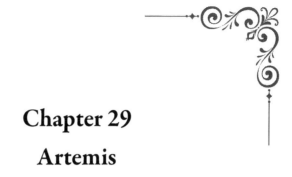

Chapter 29
Artemis

CALLISTO WAS QUIET and still lying on the ground.

Each beat of my swollen heart, hammered loudly against the quietness of hers.

I couldn't move.

"What have you done to her?"

Go away, I wanted to scream. The words were stuck in my burning throat, begging to be released. But I didn't: that's not what Hanna would have wanted.

"She's fine, she's just sleeping." My voice was raspy. "Hanna is fine. I promise, Lori."

She lunged to test her friend's heartbeat. Only then did she relax.

"Can you go call Nerea?" I asked.

"I'm not going anywhere. I'm staying here with Hanna. Also what happened to *her*?" She pointed to Loelia, still draped awkwardly over the couch.

"Oh, she had an accident. She'll revive in a few minutes."

Lori's eyes darted all around the tent: the red wine spilled on the ground, Loelia's slumped figure, the crutches abandoned on the ground.

"Is this a threesome gone wrong?" She asked at last.

"What-?"

"I mean, you look like you've been crying, my friend is sleeping and Loelia here looks dead, so I am thinking this definitely wasn't the good kind of threesome."

The first snort of laughter caught me unprepared: my shoulders shook with unexpected glee, my face contorted and I had no power to make it stop. By the time I met Lori's gaze, my laugh was erupting as explosively as a volcano from the depths of my belly and tears were pouring from my eyes.

"You know what? I'll go to call Nerea.." Lori's head walking back towards the entrance. "You have the scariest laugh I've ever heard."

SOON ENOUGH EUSACHIA came to drag away Loelia's unconscious body. Nerea stood by and offered me a quick pat on the shoulder before disappearing into the night with them.

Nerea had never been good about talking through feelings, and, for once, I did not resent her for it.

My only resentment was being left to share sleeping Hanna with her overly talky human friend.

Again.

"It's a cult isn't it?" Hanna's friend was towering over me. "We're being drawn into a cult, there's no other explanation."

Despite having apparently come to a conclusion, she was looking at me questioningly.

I looked back at her, unprepared to answer either way.

"You can't tell me, of course. None of the people who've been brainwashed know they have been. Maybe this is what's happening. Maybe Hanna's behaviour tonight was them testing a brainwashing drug. Maybe this is an experiment from the government and now we are trapped here and aliens are on their way to abduct us so we can procreate-"

"Hey, hold on," I said tentatively, trying to halt the flood of words coming from her mouth. "That's a no."

She did not relax. "I want to know what's going on, the chanting, the everybody-knows-everybody, Hanna's weird behaviour, the sheer attractiveness of all of the women in this campsite. It's weird."

"Well-"

"Wait, I know it!!" She said, her eyes scanning the place around. "Is this a reality show?"

"What's that?"

"God, Hanna was right, you are weird."

"She said that?" I asked, with a tinge of worry colouring my tone.

As if on clue, Hanna stirred in her sleep calling for Lori.

Lori turned toward her friend and caressed her forehead, "I'm here."

"Mmm."

I wanted to be the one Hanna called in her sleep. I knew it wasn't fair, but it didn't make my wish any less strong.

"You do like her a lot don't you?" Lori said, still watching me.

I didn't reply. My expression, alone, I suspected, gave it away.

"Still, I want some answers."

Lori's warning tone, from a human, in any other situation, would have angered me for days, but I had changed in the past week. And, more importantly, I knew where her concern came from. She cared for Hanna, just as I did. We were on the same team.

"I think she went a bit far with the wine," I said. The best version of the truth I could give her.

"I've seen my friend drunk enough times to know she does not go around touching random women. She does giggle a lot though."

Apparently, not *that* good of a version.

"How did you know she was in trouble?" Lori was not the kind to wait for an answer, I was learning this.

"I know Loelia. She's a bit of a player" I said.

"Oh really? So she was in danger?"

Not really, but I had to make sure."

"So just a concerned citizen regarding my friend's safety, are you? No special interest there?"

I must had a pained expression on my face because Lori's expression softened slightly.

"You were very kind to her. I'll admit it."

I shrugged.

"What's the deal with you, by the way?" She asked, again, changing the subject out of the blue.

"What do you mean?"

"What are your intention regarding my friend?" She specified. She was studying my expression as if trying to extract the truth with the brute force of her gaze.

"I like your friend, you said that yourself."

"But why? I mean, my friend is perfect and gorgeous, obviously. But my question is why is she the one you like most of all the women here. Since you are... well-" She hesitated and grimaced as she continued, "- fairly attractive. You know you could just be playing around with a bunch of women, at this moment. Hell, there is a whole campsite full of people falling about whenever you enter a room."

This was the moment I feared. I had to give to Lori the closest resemblance of truth I could muster. Or maybe not. Maybe if I waited long enough she would distract herself with more questions.

Unfortunately, Lori seemed determined to listen.

I swallowed. "What initially kept me away from her was the same thing that was pushing me to approach her: she reminded me of someone I lost a long time ago."

Lori expression told me I was doing very poorly so far.

"But then I got to meet the real Hanna. She was kind with Loelia, which I now regret seeing as a positive," I intertwined my fingers to keep my knees in place against my chest, "and then I found out about her love for the outdoors and the way she's so curious - a bit nosey, let's be honest... I discovered she despised small talk and was strong-minded and very cool headed. Her reaction in the emergency with the deer was the sexiest thing I'd seen in a long time."

"Mmmm.." Lori was clearly processing my words. "Does that mean you want to see her outside of here?"

It was a hard question. Lori and no clue what she was asking me. Giving up my God's status for seventy long years was no small sacrifice. Let alone knowing Hanna would die and her fate would always be in the hands of my Father.

"My life is in Greece.." I said, trying to explain in human's term the sacrifice such a choice required

"Then you are not good enough for my friend" She said, raising her shoulders. "I want someone who's committed to her 100%. She deserves someone who loves her, and despite my better judgement, I think she likes you enough that you could have been that for her."

"Did she tell you that?"

Goddess, I sounded like a puppy dog. Who was I kidding? I didn't really have a choice. What was I going to do? Head back on the Olympus and pretend this never happened? That ship had sailed long ago, the moment I had bled because of her. Even before that: since I had been able to open up about my past and see her eyes glinting in the dark of our tent as she told me about her life.

Lori just rolled her eyes and composed her expression into something Nerea would have been proud of. "Isn't it obvious already? God, the lesbians. Ain't nobody got any idea how complicated it is between two women."

I didn't think that she expected me to react to that.

I spent the night in the tent with Hanna and Lori. I didn't know what Aphrodite's ladies were up to, but either way, I wasn't going to sleep and let them catch us by surprise.

So I stayed awake all night, as usual. Every time Hanna made a noise or spoke a word in her sleep, I caressed her cheek, the same way I saw Lori did. I didn't want to overstep. I just wanted to soothe her. Letting her know I was here for her no matter what.

Because I would be. Whether from down here or up there, I was determined to be her protector.

Chapter 30

Hanna

I WOKE UP IN A POOL of sweat.

Some stray light of sunshine had infiltrated the tent and besieged my eyelids. I knew when to accept defeat: I screened them with my hand and opened my eyes.

Brutal.

Even my stomach was protesting.

I attempted to sit up and my vision blurred. *What happened last night?* For as much as I tried to remember, my mind drew a blank.

On the mattress next to mine laid a fully clothed Lori and at my feet stood Artemis. She was leaning against the tent's fabric walls, holding her knees, her chin tucked in. Those same annoying beams of light were playing irreverently with her ruffled hair. She looked so young and innocent under them.

Noticing my stirring, she tilted her face towards me. Her eyes, too, wrestled with the sneaky light.

"Good morning," she mouthed. Heavy bags marked her eyes, but her smile was as guileless as it had ever been.

Stupid butterflies.

She nodded towards the outside. I untangled myself from the wet sheets and followed her into the morning sunshine, careful not to wake up Lori.

"Are you alright?"

I hugged myself. "Yes, all in working order," I smiled before my eyes fell back to the ground.

"Good..good," she was shifting her weight from one foot to another, careful to avoid my eyes, too.

The sneaking suspicion that I had done something irremediably wrong gripped me.

"I really don't remember what happened last night, after the wine tasting, so if I said something terribly embarrassing... that was *awkward Hanna*." I waved my hand, "Hi, this is sober Hanna and she is normal."

My attempt at humour triggered the tiniest of smiles from the woman in front of me.

"Don't worry... you've done nothing of the sort."

"Oh well, then..-"

"But your friend Lori has threatened to sue Eusachia and the campsite and- to quote her -*make us all regret ever sending the two of you on a cult based vacation in the middle of nowhere*. So I am pretty sure she's going to want to create as much distance between you both and this place as fast as possible."

"I mean, it's been quite an eventful few days not going to lie.."

A wry smile fluttered across Artemis' lips "So you believe in the cult story?"

"Not necessarily.. but it is all a bit weird, isn't it?"

"A bit."

I watched as she worried her lip with her teeth, "So you feel good..?"

"Yes. I really do."

"I see.. I see." What I saw was her hands playing with the hem of her shirt. "You'd tell me if I did something really embarrassing though, right?"

"Of course not."

"Huh, that's reassuring."

She searched for my eyes. "You were.. very you last night. In a good way."

That really wasn't reassuring.

She shifted her weight again. "So where are you heading, next?"

"Back to the city. A few more days of vacation and then the usual work. Nothing glamorous." I intertwined my fingers to calm their nervous little dance. "Plenty of pets waiting for me there, though."

"I am sure they're in good hands."

I smiled "Should I assume you are heading back to Greece soon?"

"Looks like it." She paused and stared into my eyes. "Lots to sort through there in my absence."

"So you're leaving the campsite early too?"

"I think it got a bit too weird for my taste as well."

"Makes sense." I desperately wanted to say something else, I just had no clue what it could be.

There was silence between us when we heard the loud humming noise of Lori's awakening.

Artemis turned to go. "So maybe I'll catch you later?" I said, awkwardly offering her my hand.

She took it in her own. "Yes, of course... I was going to.. in that direction. I mean that one, actually."

"Good."

"Good-bye then." Her eyes indulged in mine a moment more.

"Yes.. good-bye."

"SO WHAT'S THE RESPONSE...Was I that bad last night?" The light and Artemis' absence had made my head thunder louder and my stomach knots tighter.

The corner of her mouth scrunched up in a mocking twist, "define bad."

"Oh God," I said, covering my face with my hands.

"Hey babe, relax. However crazy the thing was that you did, by the time I arrived you were already sleeping, so it couldn't have lasted that long."

"You left me drunk and alone with Artemis?!?"

"I'm sure there were a couple of cheesy lines, a bit of tripping over your feet and some jokes that didn't land quite as they should.... Oh and possibly a weird threesome with Loelia..? Any memories about that?"

"What the hell? No, Lori. I had no threesomes. I think. I mean, I am fairly sure" I paused, contemplating the horror. "Did Artemis looked weirded out by me? She seemed really tense earlier.."

"I am telling you that you might have had a threesome and that's your first question? Damn, you've got it worse than I thought." She sighed loudly. "No, she seemed.. sweet. Like she cared about you. In a slightly overprotective romantic way, mind."

"Huh?"

"She refused to leave the tent when I kindly tried to show her the door. She said it was for your safety. Weird attitude-"

"Seeing how the last 10 days have gone perhaps she had a point.."

"Perhaps.. But you haven't heard the best part yet," she added enthusiastically.

Now I was scared. "What is it?"

"I am second bff with Artemis now. I mean you are still number one obviously.."

"How did this even happened? That was fast, literally overnight!"

"We had a heart to heart about you and- you know how I am- I get overly excited about people. Perhaps she wouldn't call what we have a bff relationship. She'd probably call it an understanding of sorts."

"What did you talk about?!" I asked horrified. Lori was an oversharer, the kind of person who couldn't hold back if she tried. Within the first twenty-four hours of meeting her, I knew all about her, up to and including Nana, her childhood pet chinchilla. Honestly, she would have made a tremendous lesbian had she had the inclination.

"So.. the short version is that she's good for a one night stand but she's not forever material."

"Oh Dear God, did you actually interrogate her?!"

"That's what good friends do," she looked at me unapologetically, and gave me an awkward pat on my back.

I struggled to imagine Artemis withstanding the endless series of probing questions Lori had probably assault her with. Lori and I shared that trait.

"Sure, but tell what did she actually say?"

"She said that she has to go back to Greece, unfortunately, her whole life is there."

"You asked her is she planned on moving to the Uk for me?" I really wished I had my pillow with me so I could throw it at her face.

"You were the one who explained to me the whole u-hauling thing with lesbians!"

"I've known her for a week! To replant your life for someone so soon is a ridiculous ask even by lesbian standards, Lori!"

"Not for my friend" Lori said unflinching. "I've known you for a long time, Hanna. You deserve someone willing to put all of their eggs in your basket, excuse the phrasing. You are kind and beautiful and I am the luckiest friend for having you."

I felt hint of tears swelling in my eyes, " Oh Lori, how would I manage without you?"

"Don't know, don't ask," She said, holding me tighter. "Now let's get out of this place"

LORI WAS PACKING OUR bags into the car with the eagerness she usually reserved for Fleabag binges.

I was left with a wicked idea in my head. So wicked, in fact, it refused to leave my brain.

"Lori, I am going out for a second.. to breath in some fresh air while I still can."

I felt a pang of guilt for leaving her huffing and puffing alone, but I had to try.. one last time.

Very adamant that what I was about to do was embarrassing, I mustered the courage of a champion to cross the last few meters of grass separating me from the main tent.

"Hey" I said "Can we talk?"

"Of course" Artemis's head turned towards me immediately. Her eyes still bore the dark shadows, a testament to the suspiciously turbulent night that has just passed. I feared part of it might be my fault.. and Lori's, of course. But Artemis didn't seem displeased of seeing me yet again, just surprised.

"So.." I started again as we awkwardly stood in front of each other. "I wanted to apologise about last night. The way I behaved was unjustifiable."

"You remember?" She asked in shock.

"Not after Loelia's wine. But Lori's filled in a few of the gaps... a threesome?"

I thought I could see the faintest hint of a smile on her face, "pretty wild, huh?" She was joking, I could tell.

"No threesome?"

"Most definitely not a threesome."

"Then let me just thank you for taking care of me. Lori told me you were quite gentle and made sure I was sleeping fine and didn't have convulsions, or a heart attack or anything of the sort."

"My pleasure," she said simply.

"Finally I would like to clarify that when Lori asked you whether you'd be willing to move to England for me she wasn't acting on my behalf. I think she misunderstood an earlier lesson I delivered to her about the dangers of u-haul relationships. She took it as positive encouragement to ask strangers inappropriate questions."

"I think Lori was just looking out for you," she said, taking a step towards me.

"She's a good friend like that but sometimes she fails to understand that that kind of help might backfire."

"It wasn't her words.. I mean, she didn't scare me or anything.."

"I didn't mean you should have done anything different-" embarrassment heated up my face.. again.

"It's just..family responsibility back home in Greece, and you know-"

She took another step towards me, and leaned forward.

I wanted to kiss her. Hell, I wanted to do a lot more than that with her.

"...I totally understand. Really. You don't owe me an explanation, or anything."

Artemis got quiet.

"Babe, get your ass over here. We're leaving this place." Lori yelled from the car.

I begged an invisible deity for one more crumb of courage.

"Here," I said handing Artemis the piece of paper, "if you ever found yourself in England again and needed a tour guide, or something, that's my number."

She stared at the piece of paper for long enough that I feared she'd hand it back.

"No cellphones in Greece?" I joked.

"We do, I think," she said, stashing my number in her pocket.

Lori beeped the horn and the sound reverberated around the campsite. "We need to go" She yelled again.

"Well then, I wish you the best." I stuck my hand out for an awkward handshake. She was so close her scent was making me dizzy.

"You too."

I paused a second longer.

Our eyes locked.

"Hannaaa!"

I had Lori and my animals. Not to mention Mr. Ogdson, my snake plant. It was time to go back to my everyday's life. It was going to be fine.

I jumped into the car. No sooner had I climbed onto the seat than Lori locked the doors and started the engine.

"Wait Lori. I haven't said goodbye to any of the others! We have to turn around."

"No!" She yelled. "We're never going back. I said good bye to all of them on your behalf, anyway."

"Is there something you're not telling me?"

"Nope.. I am just eager to get home."

"Ok, sure." My eyes followed Artemis' figure disappearing from my view through the car window.

I had known her for ten days. It was going to be fine.

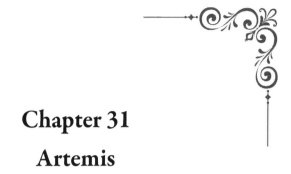

Chapter 31
Artemis

I FOLLOWED THE CAR as it wound up the pebbled road.

"Does that mean we've won, my queen?" Nerea was at my side. I had not heard her approaching.

"I suspect so."

"You don't sound as jubilant as I'd have expected given you've proven your sister's prediction wrong." Despite the casual tone, I knew Nerea: there was nothing casual about what she'd said.

"Have you taken care of the issue with Aphrodite's ladies?"

"They're now all sporting crow's feet around their eyes and mouths," she smirked. "And before you ask, yes, Loelia's ones are permanent. You'll have to be the one lifting the curse."

"Never."

"As we are all aware, my queen."

"Thank you Nerea. At last, you've done a good job."

My eyes were still fixed on the road as if the car would reappear at the edge of the meadow. "And send news to my sister that we are ready to leave."

She coughed.

"If there is something you want to say, Nerea?" I said with an impatient wave of my hand. "It's irritating to have you standing behind me quietly."

"What are we going to do now?"

"What do you mean?" I turned towards her.

"I mean, what comes next?"

"Home, of course, weren't you listening?"

"I see." Nerea was a tough player in the game of indecipherable one liners. "So you're good."

"Yes, I am good." I replied, hugging myself.

The nymph still did not move.

"Are you standing there for the sake of irritating me?" I asked."Is that the way you take revenge for my manners, Nerea?"

"You see enemies where there are none, my queen. And even if there were, you'd be the worst of all."

I turned towards her and gave her a bitter smile.

"Of all the wise things you've said Nerea, this might be the most worthy of chocolate wrappers."

"What's that?"

"Never mind Nerea. It's all good."

"Ready to go?" She asked.

I unwrapped the bandage and notice the wound had healed almost completely. I'd made the right choice after all. "Yes, let's go," I said at last.

I SPENT THE FIRST FEW days back in Olympus restless. The nymphs were clumsily attempting to soothe me, to little avail.

"Perhaps more ambrosia?"

"I have drunk enough ambrosia to turn me gold," I said, turning Amnisiades away.

Neither Athena nor Aphrodite had yet came back from their earthly expeditions.

Normally, I would be pleased about this, as it meant I was winning. But there were just so many questions bubbling under the surface of their absences.

Why were they taking so long? Was it a trick to get in my head? A way to test my resolution? Not that I was in danger of doubting my decision. Not at all.

"None of that, my queen," Nerea would answer patiently whenever I asked.

My sisters hated Earth. Aphrodite at least. Athena was probably enjoying playing with her new human toys.

"My queen, everything is proceeding according to plan. Their delay is a good thing."

"Then why did Aphrodite's spell let Hanna and I leave the place earlier?"

"How many times have we gone through this?"

"One more time, Nerea, please!"

"It's because even Aphrodite knows you can't force love. Her set up counted on the fact that after a few days you'd naturally gravitate towards each other to the point neither of you would want to leave. She did not count on either of you having true desire to leave the campsite."

I shook my head, my feet tapping on the mosaic floor, "She's still playing with my mind, Nerea. I can tell."

Nerea did not answer and left the room.

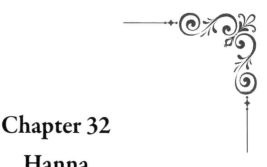

Chapter 32
Hanna

"GREAT NEWS!" LORI SAID bursting through the door and waving a piece of paper in the air. "I got a job."

She had dressed up for the interview. The navy blue blazer emphasised her eyes.

"Wait is that *my* blazer?"

"It's your contribution to me leaving your apartment at last," she said pirouetting around the room.

"You are leaving?"

"Yes.. finally!" she said. Her smile dimmed as she looked at me "I thought you'd be happy. I've been squatting at your place for weeks, I thought you valued the quiet."

"I do, it's just.. there's no pressure for you to go anywhere. I don't mind at all."

"I know, babe. But it is time for this birdie to fly," she jiggled her hands. "Now, ask me about the job."

"Yes. Right. What is the job?"

Past experience suggested it could be anything: a professional cat cuddler, a real life model for an art school, a mattress tester. The sky was the limit.

"... Surveys!"

I'll admit, I was a bit underwhelmed. 'Millenial-leaning-against-a-wardrobe-in-a-furniture-catalogue' was a tough gig to follow.

"Sounds good!"

"I get to ask people questions. All-day-long. Isn't it great?!"

"Yes. Yes! It's great!" I went to hug her, "Lori, I am very happy for you. It's so amazing!"

"I know. I was born for this."

I was wearing my three day old pyjamas and next to Lori's career-woman look, I felt severely underdressed. I rushed back to my curled up position on the sofa.

"So," she said plopping back next to me. "How are you doing today?"

"Great. I'm doing great." I replied, handing her the remote. "Want crisps?"

"Nah. Being in touch with nature has awakened a deep need for unprocessed food in my body." She said unwrapping an all-natural-and-organic bar she'd fished from her back pocket. "Want to share?"

"I'm still a heathen," I said, picking up the packet of crisps.

"So.. have you left the house, yet?"

"Not really. The sofa is too comfy."

"That's not really normal behaviour for you, though, isn't it?"

For all of her supposed carelessness, Lori had a disarming ability to get straight to the point. Today her words cut me like a focused and merciless assassin.

"I got a free week's vacation. That's not normal for me either."

Lori stared in my eyes with her surgical gaze "There is something else, though, isn't there?"

"I don't know what you mean..-"

"You've met somebody."

I stuffed my mouth with crisps and shook my head.

"So that's a yes.. Wait.Three days...This is about Artemis, isn't it?"

"What?! Don't be ridiculous. I'm not thinking of her. Why would I even-? I knew her for a week, Lori! You don't believe me capable of getting so attached to someone in just seven days, do you?"

Lori's mouth had shrunk into a thin line. She bit her lip, "I severely misunderstood the situation," she said, pensive. "I thought she was just the kind of attractive woman that tickled your fancies.. if you know what I mean.."

"Don't be gross, Lori"

"So it's a crush. A proper one?"

"Maybe. I mean no. It's probably just the fact that she's so damn attractive."

"So yes. It's a proper crush. I got this." She rubbed her hands "Do we know anything about her.. instagram? Facebook? Number?"

I shook my head.

"Date of birth?" She asked with a dismayed expression.

I stayed quiet.

"Full name, at least?"

I fell back on the sofa and sighed, "I told you it was stupid."

"Hey," Lori grabbed my hand. "It's not stupid. Maybe this is less about Artemis herself and more about what it means.. Maybe it is nature's way of telling you you're ready to meet someone and fall in love again. Either way I think it's time you admitted something.."

I looked at her, perplexed.

"You have a type. I am not swiping right on any more lipstick lesbians on your behalf."

I curled the corner of my mouth in my best impression of a smile, "fair enough."

We both watched in silence as colourful people passed through the silent TV..

"Lori, I have another confession."

"Oh no..."

"I gave her my number."

"And she hasn't called?"

I shook my head.

"Damn, I thought she was smarter than that."

"She probably has dozens of women throwing themselves at her at this very minute.. I was just stupid for thinking I had a chance. I mean, you saw her-"

"If you don't stop right now I am never giving you the blazer back."

"Would you have?"

"Yes, at least for tonight. We're going out." She put a hand in front of my mouth "Shhh. We are. So shut up and get ready."

I looked at her dejected. I had no energy to fight back.

Chapter 33
Artemis

"YOU'RE BACK AND YOU didn't come over to say hi?" Dionysus opened his arms, hugging several inches of air.

I didn't want to engage with that.

"Hi, cousin," I said, shooting another look down on Earth. Hanna was fine. I relaxed my shoulders.

"I'm offended, little one. I bet a few souls with Ares on you staying down there."

I scoffed. "Should have bet the other way then."

"So...someone is having a bad day," he said, carving a space on the lounging chair with his hips.

"I don't do feelings, not anymore, Diony. Talking about them, analysing them, inspecting them. It doesn't agree with me."

The annoying smirk on his face gave away his skepticism. "What about crying them out? Is that out of style too?"

"It was one time. One," I said testily. "How is that everyone is so quick to remember my weaknesses, but they all suffer permanent memory loss when it comes to my achievements?"

In answer, Dionysus produced a cup of ambrosia and gulped it down quickly. "Maybe that's the problem.. You were the fiercest of us all. I believe Zeus himself feared you. Really, you're lucky there was no prophecy about you taking over, because he would have found a way to end you."

I stole the cup from his hand and raised it in the air, "to fatherly love!" A new wave of amber liquid filled the cup and I downed it all.

Dionysus nodded, a sad smile on his face.

I wiped my mouth and thumped the golden cup against the banquet's wooden table. "I'm still fierce. I'm still dangerous."

"You showed your weakness, Artemis. There is no coming back from that."

"So what am I supposed to do, huh? A mass murder? An official statement?" I slumped against the soft velvet surface. "I am well on my way to winning the bet. Does that account for something?"

He shook his head unhappily. "You're looking at it all wrong."

I plopped down on my elbow, "Don't give me that stagshit about embracing it." I stared at him in anger, "I am not going to cuddle kittens and draw rainbows."

"If you don't care about my opinion, then why do you ask me what you should do?"

I passed him the cup, "I care about your opinion, Diony. That's why I haven't chased you out of the room with an arrow, yet."

"Uuhhh... scary." He jiggled his hand in the air.

It stole a smile from my lips, "so.. what should I do?"

"Wrong question, Artis." He pointed his finger at me, threateningly. "Why do you care so much about what the rest of the Olympians think?"

"They are my family. Dysfunctional, toxic, problematic... but they are the only one of my kind. I'd be alone without them."

"What about me? What about your sisters? You always liked Persephone and Hades. And Ares bet for your victory in this latest venture." He waved his fingers in the air. "As I see it there is truly only one piece of stagshit-as you'd call him- walking these halls. And you've decided how you feel about all of us based on his betrayal."

"But none of you fear me."

"And what does fear has to do with love?" Dionysus shook his head again. "My wife feared me but she did not love me. I'm still here drinking ambrosia and wine, as I did before I met her, but now I'm not searching for ecstasy, I'm drowning my pain."

"Arianna.."

"I knew her heart belonged to Teseo, but I thought -when she accepted to marry me - that that coward of a man was long gone from her mind. I had not realised how much she feared the wrath of a God." His hands were shaking. "I loved her, Artemis. And loving her did not make me any less of a God."

He gripped my wrist. His eyes were misty. "I never regretted it. I never even skinned Teseo alive as I imagined doing so many times, because of how she felt about him. Love is timeless, and all forgiving. Two millennials I've been in pain, just like you, and I'd give up my divinity anytime if it meant she could love me back for a day."

I looked down on the ground, shame keeping me from looking straight into his eyes, "I miss her."

"I know. Even by your standards, the past few days' behaviour has been over the top.."

I sipped more ambrosia. "I can't loose my divinity."

"Why not?" he pleaded.

"Because I can't be powerless. Otherwise.. I'm left with nothing."

Dionysus shook his head violently "You are left with a chance."

"A chance to be betrayed again by my Father? A chance for any of the Olympians to take advantage of my weaknesses?"

"A chance at happiness, Artemis." He said taking the cup of ambrosia from my hand. "One you need desperately."

I PACED THE HALL BACK and forth, from the north window down to the banquet, thousands of times after Dionysus had left.

Happiness.

A weird concept, wasn't it?

I looked down on Earth. Hanna, tiny and weak in the world down below, was at home laying in her small apartment.

She had no idea who I truly was or what I'd have to give up for her.

I had two hours left until the definitive win and neither of my sisters were back. Athena had sent word to the nymphs two days ago about her return, but then... nothing. Aphrodite, instead, had completely disappeared.

Did it matter what their decision was, if I didn't even know my own?

I searched my pockets. The white piece of paper Hanna had given me was still in one of them, the blue ink smudged on the final digit: 3.

But the human contraption -*the cillphone*- the object that had put me in this mess in the first place, was nowhere to be found.

Only one person on the whole of Olympus who could have taken it.

I dashed through the long corridors and burst into Athena's chambers. On the wall, arranged in perfect rows stood all manners of human contraptions. All rectangular, all with a mirror surface, all labeled with their respective year of invention. 4,002,256,342. 4,002,256,343, 4,002,256,344.

I grabbed the one that most resembled the original. The edges were round and its surface covered my entire hand. I pressed the central button and it came to life.

One by one I touched the numbers on the paper.

Nothing happened.

I was a Goddess for Zeus' sake! How was it so hard?

"Need help?"

Nerea's voice made me jump.

"I was just -" I swallowed. The human thing -cellphone, Athena's display suggested- was in my hand, blinking wildly in Nerea's direction.

She rolled her eyes. "I know exactly what you were doing, my queen." She grabbed it from my hand and clicked a few buttons.

"You write your message here."

"How do you know this?" I was pretty sure Nerea was as ignorant as me when it came to human inventions.

"I asked your sister to teach me before she left, just in case."

I shot her a look.

"I'm not apologising," she said crossing her arms over her chest.

Dear Hanna,

I wish to stay with you on Earth, until your mortal death.

Nerea peeked over my shoulder "You can't write that, " her expression was contorted in shock.

"It's poetic and truthful, what's wrong with that?"

She sighed. "People do dates now. Not declaration of love. You have to ask her out somewhere: dinner, movies, mini golf. Something relaxed."

I scoffed. "My idea is better."

"If you want her to run away from you screaming.. sure."

"Fine, tell me what I should say," I grumbled.

Dear Hanna,

I would like to invite you out for dinner one of these days. In a restaurant. Let me know the time that would best suit you.

Nerea stole the cellphone from my hand again.

If you'll have me, of course.

Artemis.

"It's implied" I protested.

She did not argue back, instead she just pressed the arrow. "There you go."

"Sent?"

"Sent."

We dashed to the window and looked down.

I watched as Hanna grabbed the phone. She stared at the message in confusion and then, apparently understanding, she smiled.

My breath snagged in my throat.

Through the luminous screen, happiness blinked at me.

Yes, I'll have you.

Chapter 34

Hanna

I stood in front of the mirror, inspecting the way the flowery dress fell over my hips with a skeptical look.

"Are you sure this is the one?"

"You'd need to be blind to not be sure that this is the one."

A pile of dresses was towering on the bed, like leftovers of an imagined *plain Jane* to *beauty queen* reality tv show contest. Lori had waited patiently for me to wear each one of those and at last, when I'd come into the room wearing the current flowy dress, she'd made The Face. "She's going to drop dead on the floor. No-better- she's going to tell you she moved to England for you and *then* drop on the floor.."

"I put on too much lipstick. "I hesitated. "Yes, I did. I am going to go wipe it off."

Lori halted between me and the bathroom door. "You're not going to take off anything. Look at you!" She exclaimed with a swiping gesture from my head up to my heel clad feet. "You look like a beautiful, sparkly, sophisticated... Goddess. Artemis won't even begin to imagine the sheer luck she had the day you decided to give her a chance."

The ring bell rang.

Oh God. Oh God. I can't do this.

"You can do this," Lori said with a wink, before disappearing down the stairs. "Yes," I heard her answer the intercom, "you can come in. But you've got to behave."

Oh God.

I rushed down the stairs before Lori got any weird ideas about recreating a prom night. Her disappointed look, when she saw me in the living room, told me I'd made the right choice.

I shot a quick look at the clock in the corner. Just one minute before seven, Artemis was right on time. The room seemed to have shrunk in size, my stomach was trembling and I kept shuffling from foot to foot while waiting for the swaggering beauty to appear at the door.

Would she like the dress? Maybe she'd prefer me in trousers, in a power woman look.

Maybe this was a pity invite and it had been a very stupid idea to accept..

I heard the heavy footsteps climbing the stairs and jumped toward the door before Lori could.

I opened it with a tremulous smile and..

"Hanna. I am so sorry. Please."

Finley.

I hadn't seen her in a year. Not since I'd caught her in the throws of passion with her colleague in our house, our bed.

I was speechless.

She was surprised too, judging by the thorough look she gave me. "Going somewhere?" Her usual smirk was not quite as captivating as I remembered.

"Finley-"

"You look stunning," she said, trying to edge inside.

As a reflex, I pulled the handle towards me, reducing the entrance space. "This is not a good moment. Actually, there are no good moments at all."

"Calling your date with your ex's name is not a great start babe..-ohh" Lori had peeked through the door and fell quiet when she saw the woman standing on our doormat.

"You need to leave," I said firmly.

"You don't really mean it, c'mon," Finley leaned on the doorframe. Her half-sleeve was on full display under the electric light of the building. I wished she'd move away so I could slam the door in her face and grab my purse.

"Baby, you've got to understand. We were together for such a long time.. one moment of weakness is something you could easily forgive.."

I knew I wasn't supposed to engage with her. I knew it.

Lori behind me, though, had other plans "What did you say? How dare you?!" She pointed her finger at Finley with such force that she made the woman with a religious crossfit obsession retreat down two whole steps.

"Lori, you must know, I thought of her all year." Finley's tone was pleading, as overdramatic as her shenanigans usually were. "Hanna," she turned towards me, all puppy eyes and sweetness, "I missed you everyday."

Of course, on none of those days had she bothered to send a text or call. I kept quiet, though. Disagreeing with Finley, in my experience, meant only being trapped in a argument. Best case scenario, it lead nowhere; worst case scenario, it lead to me apologising. "Finley, I told you I need to go. Please leave."

"Baby," she caught my eyes. "You've got to give us another chance."

Lori, still behind me, was fuming. She was tapping her feet incessantly against the floor but she kept quiet this time, following my lead for once.

"Look, baby, I'm telling you I've changed-"

My favourite ruffled hair appeared at the bottom of the staircase right at that moment.

Artemis' smile, timid and uncertain at first, died on her lips as she took in the scene above her. For a moment I feared she would up and run and never look back.

Instead, she steeled her gaze and took a few steps towards us.

"Hi there, you must be the one who's trying to steal my girlfriend away," Finley greeted her with an over-the-top gesture.

Artemis stood agonisingly still for a second.

"Artemis, it's not like you think. She's not my girlfriend. She's-"

I saw the cloud of doubt crossing my date's eyes. It was over, wasn't it?

And then, unexpectedly, Artemis extended her hand, "Finley, isn't it?"

"Oh, so she's told you about me?" Despite her best efforts, Finley's relaxed demeanour had been shaken by Artemis' words. She looked like a scared puppy with Artemis towering a few good inches above her.

I gave a relieved sigh "Yes. My inopportune ex. Who was about to leave," I said, pointedly.

"..you could come with me," Finley insisted.

Really, an angry God was the only explanation for this mess. I still half expected Artemis to pull one of her burning looks, reacting to Finley inflammatory attitude like a fire to kindling. I could already see this whole night turn into a disaster right here, before I had even had a chance to leave the house.

But Artemis surprised me once more. She stepped to one side and looked deep into my eyes. Hypnotising. That's what she was.

A smile spread to her lips but did not quite reach her eyes, "I'll be here in whatever way you'll have me, Hanna." She said, ignoring Finley and her silly Hawaiian shirt. "I'm holding my promise. So if this is not a good moment, or you've changed your mind. I will wait until you're ready and enthusiastic. Should that moment ever come again."

I could have kissed her right there on the house threshold, in front of Lori and Finley and the buzzing lights of the corridor. But I had better plans for that, later. Again and again with any of luck.

I bit my lips and smiled at her, "I said I'll have you, and I, too, am a woman of my word."

The smile that grew on her lips left me hopelessly anchored. No one moved as Artemis and I stood, staring into each other's eyes.

"Your purse.." Lori finally said, offering me the small blue bag.

"Hanna, wait," Finley still wasn't done apparently.

Artemis stepped towards her. My breath hitched. *Oh God.* " It's time to let go, Finley," was all she said. There was no aggression to her tone, no veiled threat or menace. "Whatever guilt, whatever unsaid words, whatever it is you are trying to prove, trust me, you have to let go."

Finley, too, must have known. Because instead of her usual bravado and biting tongue, she kept quiet.

I took that chance to slip past her and reach for Artemis' arm. My hand closed around it and I felt her strong muscles flex under my fingertips. Her eyes were still burning through mine.

"Let's go."

She gave me a crooked smile back, "yes, let's go."

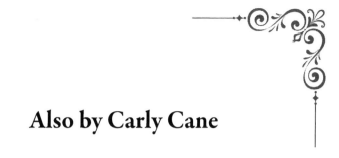

Also by Carly Cane

Queer Olympus Goddesses series:

Artemis and The Dating App[1]
Athena and The College Professor[2]
Aphrodite and The Reality Show[3]

1. https://www.amazon.com/Artemis-Dating-Queer-Olympus-Goddesses-ebook/dp/
B082H46YLC/ref=sr_1_1?keywords=Artemis+and+The+Dat-
ing+app&qid=1582393529&sr=8-1

2. https://www.amazon.com/dp/B083ZMR517?ref_=pe_3052080_276849420

3. https://www.amazon.com/dp/B08526L1NK/ref=sr_1_2?keywords=Aphrodite+and+the+re-
ality+show&qid=1582392985&sr=8-2

About the Author

H ello, fellow human :)
    Thank you for reading to the end of this book! This is my first project to make it to the publishing stage, and so, as all first kids are, it is also my favourite. (JK, sis.)

None of it could have happened without the wonderful people in my life, from the encouraging yes-you-can-do-it! friends to the this-makes-no-sense-it-needs-to-go beta readers.

And, of course, my family, who, surprisingly, did not bat an eye when I told them I was going to be a writer.

You rock, family.

But since this book is for you, reader, get in touch and let me know what you think at:

(I AM ALSO CURIOUS TO know who your favourite character is since some of them are begging me for a spin off...)

---

1. https://www.facebook.com/carly.cane.754

Printed in Great Britain
by Amazon

36397631R00101